~~MERRY~~ *Creepy* CHRISTMAS

12 Twisted Tales

2023

FROM BLACK MARE BOOKS

Contents

THE CHRISTMAS PONY

By Artemis Greenleaf

VIOLET and Alison peered into the shop window. Evergreen garland, trimmed with red velvet bows, framed the plate-glass window. A brightly colored electric train ran around the circumference of the display window, drawing the eyes of passersby.

"Gran! Would you look at this!" Alison jumped up and down, pointing to the black and white pinto rocking horse featured in the display.

"It's lovely," the girls' grandmother replied.

"Can we go in and have a look?" Violet asked, her eyes beseeching.

"Only a look, girls. I expect it's very expensive. Looks like an antique."

The two girls rushed into the boutique, nearly bowling over a frazzled woman with an armload of shopping bags.

"Sorry." Gran gave the woman a tense smile.

She nodded wearily and trudged out of the shop.

Alison and Violet stood in front of the display, smitten by the carved wooden horse. Its glossy black, real horsehair mane flowed down past the bottom edge of its neck, and the same kind of red bow that graced the garland was clipped into the forelock that covered its huge glass eyes.

"I would name her Blaze." Alison nodded matter-of-factly.

Violet cocked her head toward her younger sister. "Too common. I know you're just in second grade, Allie, but you have to agree—she needs a more regal name."

"Queenie?"

"No." Violet thought for a moment. "What about Zephyr? That's the name of the West Wind. I bet she could fly like the wind. If she were a real pony."

"Oh, she could take you anywhere you can imagine, as fast as you please." The shopkeeper, a scrawny man with a few limp hairs combed across the top of his head, suddenly appeared beside them.

The girls recoiled and scurried to their grandmother.

"Imagination is a powerful thing, indeed." Gran said, a hand on each girl's shoulder.

A greasy smile seeped across the proprietor's over-wide mouth. "No imagination required." He patted the horse's worn saddle. "Just sit on the horse, think it, and you're there."

Gran raised an eyebrow. "Alas, we shall have to take you at your word. Come on, girls. We've got to go and meet your mother."

"She's on sale. Rock bottom price."

Violet turned back to the shopkeeper. "How much?"

He raised his hands. "Oh, never mind. Your grandmamá is in a hurry. Zephyr here needs a special owner. Someone who has time to get to know her. She isn't just some ordinary object to be snatched off the shelf, stuffed in a bag, and carried off."

Gran rubbed the bridge of her nose. *Had his Christmas Eve sales been so slow that he was smarming a ten-year old?*

Alison also turned to the wiry man.

He tipped his head toward the rocking horse. "Give her a little pat."

Both girls reached tentatively into the display. Violet stroked a painted wooden cheek and Alison combed her fingers through the silky mane.

"Girls? We're the last ones in the shop. I'm sure they'd like to close up and get home to their families."

"We don't close for another five minutes," the proprietor assured her.

She scowled back at him.

"How much did you say, mister?" Violet looked up from the horse's delicately carved face.

He put his hands on the tops of his thighs and bent at the hip until his eyes were level with hers. "Well…." He reached out and patted the saddle again. "If, and only if, Zephyr wants to go home with you, and because it's Christmas Eve, I would consider letting her go for a very, very special price."

Both girls' eyes widened.

Gran's eyes rolled. *$1,000? $500?* She was no antiques expert, but the horse looked very similar to a hand-carved Victorian era carousel horse her cousin had bought. And she'd paid a pretty penny for that. If it wasn't an original, it was an excellent reproduction.

"What do you think, my beauty?" The shopkeeper put his hands on the sides of the horse's face. "Do you like these girls?"

"What does she say?" Alison squirmed next to her sister.

"Oh, she likes you very much." He grinned. "Very much indeed."

"Girls, I'm sure our five minutes are up."

"One dollar."

The three shoppers turned to the man.

"What did you say?" Gran slid her purse back up to her shoulder.

"One dollar. A single portrait of George Washington."

Gran cocked her head to one side, then the other. "What's the catch?"

The shopkeeper's hand flew to his chest. "Catch?"

"Gran, it's a great price. Mom can't be mad if it's only a dollar. I have my allowance money—I could pay for it."

"Violet, darling. If something sounds too good to be true, it is. Besides, how would we get it home? It's huge."

Alison jerked her hand away from the horse's mane. "What if it's haunted?"

The proprietor laughed. "Haunted! I can assure you that she is absolutely not haunted. Guaranteed. That's quite the imagination you've got there, young lady." He pushed on the horse's neck, causing it to rock back and forth. "We offer free delivery. Zephyr here can be at your house before midnight tonight."

"Please, Gran?" both girls begged.

She looked at the rocking horse, then back to her granddaughters. She turned and studied the shopkeeper. "Let me get a picture of you, with the horse."

He grinned. "Of course!"

Gran took a picture of him holding the horse's reins.

If it turns out he's got the real cashier tied up in the back and is just taking the money, I'll have a photo for the police.

The girls stayed with Zephyr, cooing and giggling, while Gran and the proprietor wound their way through the cluttered aisles to the register.

"That will be one dollar even. Cash."

Gran glanced over both shoulders before she reached into her purse for her wallet. She had to move the lab work orders she'd gotten from her doctor earlier in the week out of the way to get to it. "No tax?"

"No, ma'am." He took the bill from her hand. "All sales are final. No refunds, no returns."

She tucked a lock of hair behind her ear. "Make sure you give me a receipt, anyway."

"Of course, of course." He handed her the printout from the cash register, a form, and a pen. "Please fill this out for me so we can get her delivered. One less thing for Santa to do tonight."

Gran took the pen and filled out the form. When she went to hand it back, he looked down at it for a moment.

"There is one thing you should know."

"I knew it."

"What I said was true. That rocking horse will take you anywhere you want to go in the blink of an eye. But you have to sell her in exactly one year for exactly one dollar less than you paid for her. And you can't give her away for free."

Gran raised a skeptical eyebrow. "And what happens if I don't?"

"She'll take your soul away to where she was created."

"Sure. And where's that?"

"No one knows. This horse has been passed around for so long that knowledge is lost."

Shaking her head, Gran headed to the front of the store to collect her granddaughters.

"Good luck!" the shopkeeper called after her.

It was half-way through summer break, and the girls got to sleep in a little later than normal. They made up for it by staying up later. Alison and Violet crept down the stairs. The playroom was dark, but they didn't need light to find Zephyr. Both girls climbed onto the sturdy wooden horse and began to rock.

"Where should we go tonight, Allie?" Violet whispered.

"How about... the Big Rock Candy Mountains? We learned that song in day camp last week."

Alison clutched her sister's waist and Violet twined her fingers in the horse's mane. "Oh, Zephyr, Zephyr, brave and strong. Take us to the place we long. The Big Rock Candy Mountains."

Blue and purple lights flashed and swirled. They found themselves in a valley. The grass was soft and green. On either side, the sun glinted off transparent mountains. Trees filled with all kinds of fruits grew right up to the shoulders of the peaks.

They dismounted and gave Zephyr a pat before skipping off to explore. When they'd had their fill of sipping lemonade from the mountain streams, picking blueberry muffins from the array of bushes, and sliding down the crystal sugar slopes, they waddled back to the rocking horse and climbed aboard.

Violet patted her wooden neck. "Zephyr, Zephyr we did roam. Now we're tired, please take us home."

Yellow and orange lights flashed this time, and in a moment, they were back in the playroom.

Both girls kissed her wooden muzzle and slipped silently back up the stairs.

In the morning, neither girl was quick to rise, and they yawned all the way down the stairs for breakfast.

When they arrived in the kitchen, their mother was pulling a blue satin turban onto Gran's bald head.

Violet threw her arms around her grandmother. "How are you feeling today?"

"I'm a little better." She smiled as Alison piled on with her own hug.

The girls' mother picked up her coffee mug. "I'll be in my office."

As soon as she was out of earshot, Alison whispered, "Guess where we went last night?"

Gran leaned forward. "Where?"

"The Rock Candy Mountains!" both girls said in unison.

They spent the next half hour telling her about their adventures there, and the three of them giggled together.

After lunch, Violet and Alison left for their swimming lesson, and Gran was alone in the house. She wandered into the playroom and regarded Zephyr. "A few more months, my girl, Then we shall see what we shall see."

Gran blinked and shook her head. Must be the medication playing tricks. That wooden horse did not just flick an ear.

December had started on a bleak note. Cold mist shrouded the morning, and rain set in before noon. The family had not put up their Christmas decorations. No one was in the mood, not even on Christmas Eve.

Gran lay in a hospital bed in the living room. A hospice nurse had been visiting every day. Evaluating her condition. It was the dead of night and she heard soft footsteps on the stairs.

"Violet? Alison?"

The footfalls stopped.

"Come here, girls. It's all right."

Sheepishly they crept to her side.

"Can you help me with this bed railing? I want to see Zephyr."

"Are you sure, Gran?" Violet's voice was nearly inaudible.

"Yes."

Gran hobbled across to the playroom and plopped into a chair. The girls pushed the wooden horse over to her. She laid her hand across the saddle and whispered, "Zephyr, Zephyr, brave and strong, take me to the place I long. Across the Veil."

Blue and purple lights flashed, and Gran found herself standing in a dark, empty place. A filmy, cobweb-colored curtain shimmered next to her.

Instead of a wooden rocking horse, a black and white beast in the approximate form of a horse stood on her other side. Its eyes glowed red and wisps of smoke rose from its nostrils. The black mane and tail were no longer glossy hair, but slimy tendrils that writhed of their own accord. The creature towered on legs seemingly too long and thin to support its bulk.

Gran touched the curtain, and it rippled like a silvery liquid. She turned to the creature. "You cannot cross it, can you."

The beast tossed its great head, jostling the slithering mass between its ears. "You know I cannot."

The old woman laughed. "But I can. And I will. It's my time, after all."

The thing that had once been Zephyr stretched its long neck down toward Gran, its smoldering eyes the same height as hers. "You owe me. One soul. You agreed to the terms."

"Where is it you want to take me?"

A deep thrumming growl was the only response.

"It's been so long you've forgotten yourself. If the agreement is broken, I think the curse will also break, and you'll be returned to what you were before all this started."

The glowing eyes flared brighter, and the lower jaw opened, revealing row after row of shark-like teeth.

"Catch me if you can!" Gran leaped through the Veil.

The beast roared in impotent fury.

"What on Earth!" Violet and Alison's father stood in the door to the playroom, gaping.

Their mother stopped to see what he was talking about. "How did…? Girls!"

Cowering, Alison and Violet approached their parents.

Fear turned to delight as they spotted a black and white pony, which neighed when it saw them.

In their excitement, the girls didn't notice Gran slumped in the chair, a smile on her pale, still face.

A Helping Hand

By A. B. Richards

*W*ILL *it hurt?* The sound of the river rushing below soothes some of the jagged edges of dread from me, but not most of them.

To my left, office buildings glow red and green with holiday lights. Plastic wreaths and garlands dangle above the sleepy streets from steel cables strung across each city block downtown. One skyscraper has office lights strategically turned on to form a blocky Christmas tree.

I hate Christmas with the heat of a thousand suns. Used to love it. Not anymore. I grip the ice-slick railing on the bridge, considering my options for the most efficient way over it.

"Nice night for a walk."

A man in sweats and an orange puffy coat approaches me.

Shrugging, I look back down. "Yeah."

I fix my eyes on the water, waiting for him to pass. Instead, he stops next to me, crossing his arms and resting his elbows on the chest-high railing.

"Rough night?" he asks.

"Yeah."

"Me, too. I lost my entire family last year."

"Sorry to hear that." Maybe he has the same plan as I do. I almost laugh, imagining us helping each other over the railing and jumping together.

I wait for him to tell me more, but he says nothing. Minutes pass, and words bubble up inside of me to fill the awkward silence.

"Christmas used to be my favorite holiday. Until last year. Had to quit my job. Made me physically sick to go in."

"Hmmmm." He takes a deep breath. "What did you do?"

I fiddled with the hem of my shirt, not wanting to continue the conversation, but feeling obligated since I had started it. "Worked for a non-profit. We had a fill-Santa's-Sack drive every year and then we delivered boxes of food and gifts to people in need." I shake my head. "The way those kids' eyes lit up when they saw they were going to get something for Christmas after all."

"And you liked that?"

"Loved it. Who wouldn't like that? Being the white knight to ride in with food for the hungry and presents for the forgotten. It wasn't just kids. Old people with no family are maybe even more grateful than the little ones."

"Sounds like it was very rewarding. But then you quit. Why?"

I shiver and rub my arms. Not planning to be out here long, I'd left my coat at home in the box marked for donation to the homeless shelter. "My shrink used to ask me that. What about you? You must be lonely at Christmas."

"Yeah. Although it was never my favorite holiday. Too stressful." He cast his eyes over the rushing water below. "But it's been hard being alone. Hey, you look cold. There's an all-night diner coupla blocks that way. You want to go for a coffee?"

I can always come back later. Bridge would still be here. Maybe I can offer this man a shoulder to cry on in the meantime, my final act of holiday good will. "Sure. Lead the way."

The windows of Pop's Diner are grimy, but the inside is clean, although a little shabby. We take a booth by the window, where the sun has faded the red vinyl of the seats to a speckled pink. Dusty classic rock album covers stick haphazardly to the walls in lieu of paintings or photos. I can almost feel my skin breaking out from the bacon grease that saturates the air as we slide in opposite each other.

The waitress tucks a lock of bottle-blonde hair behind her ear and hands us each an oversized laminated menu. "Drinks?"

The man smiles at her, glancing at her name tag. "Pot of coffee, Caitlyn."

I can probably afford a cup of coffee and a tip. But nothing else. "I'd like some water, please."

She nods and turns toward the kitchen.

I move the paper napkin-wrapped silverware over a few inches. "We, uh haven't been introduced. I'm Stacey."

He nods and smiles at me. "Chad."

Caitlyn returns with the drink order and sets the coffee in the middle of the table before giving us each a glass of water and a mug. "Pie of the day is blueberry." Then she pulls a pad and the nub of a pencil from a pocket in her apron and looks at us expectantly.

"Oh, I'm—"

Chad raises his menu. "Get whatever you want, Stacey. My treat."

I really wouldn't mind having some hot food that wasn't instant ramen. I pick the cheapest thing on the menu—eggs on toast with a side of hash browns.

"Oh, come on, Stace. You have to get pie." Chad lays his menu flat.

"Fine. And a slice of blueberry pie."

He orders the large portion of steak and eggs, and the requisite dessert.

Caitlyn leaves to turn in our order and Chad pours us each a cup of coffee. "I've told you about losing my family. What happened to you? What made you hate Christmas?"

His eyes are the color of brown sugar, with little threads of gold around the edges. Soft eyes. Friendly eyes. The touches of grey around his temples make him look fatherly.

I finish stirring cream and sugar into my cup and take a long drink. "It's not something I like to talk about."

He raises his mug of black coffee. "Might make you feel better if you do."

Dr. Lometa told me that in our sessions. But I hadn't been able to pay her for some time now. "Maybe."

Chad drinks his coffee and looks out the grubby window while I fidget with the plastic stirrer.

The long silence is a vacuum that eventually pulls the story out of me. "You remember I said I worked for a non-profit? And we delivered holiday treats?"

He nods.

"Well, we usually went out in teams of two or three to drop off the packages. There was a bug going around the office and we were short staffed. My regular delivery partner was out sick, and it was the last day of services before Christmas. There were still four families left. Couldn't leave them without Christmas when there were packages sitting right there in the warehouse for them. So I made the deliveries by myself."

"I'm sure they appreciated that." Chad rests his elbows on the table.

"Oh, they did. But because I was hauling everything alone, it took longer than usual. By the time I got to the last house, I was over an hour late and it was getting dark."

"You could have gotten robbed."

"You know, I've never had that problem. There are always a few rotten apples, but most of the time, neighbors look out for each other. Even in bad neighborhoods. So, while I kept an eye on my surroundings, I wasn't really worried."

Caitlyn returns with our food, and I marvel at the speed of service. Salty, crispy, fried potatoes. Starchy comfort food that is more about feelings than fullness, a cheerful hit of carb-fueled dopamine. Maybe this diner detour is just what I needed.

"I'll bet that last family was glad to see you, even if you were late." A little smile plays on his lips, and I try to smile back, even though nausea roils my stomach.

"No." I shake my head and swallow. "I knocked on the door and it swung open. Hadn't been closed all the way. So I stepped inside and started calling out for Mrs. Robinson. The lights were all on, but she didn't answer."

Chad leans forward. "What was that like?"

I pick up my coffee mug and find it empty. I fill the cup, then add sugar. The cream takes it all the way to the brim, and some sloshes over the sides when I stir. I sip enough out of it that I can lift the cup without spilling, then hold the warm drink against my chest.

"At first, I thought maybe they were out in the back yard or something. I wasn't too worried. I just kept calling for Mrs. Robinson. Something smelled really bad in the house, though. Almost like dirty diapers wrapped in tinfoil. I didn't know…." I can't help the tear that rolls down my cheek.

"Did she hurt you?"

I close my eyes and shake my head. "When… when I went into the living room—" A sob forces its way out and I put the coffee down, hiding my face in my hands.

Chad reaches over and rubs my arm.

I struggle for control and when I feel my voice won't break, I start again. "They were in the living room. The mom and the four kids."

"Doing what?"

"They were dead."

He tilts his head and raises his hands, palm up. "Dead? Like from a gas leak?"

I shake my head and cover my mouth, jostling the coffee mug and spilling some across the table. "No. They had been stabbed, like dozens of times. Then he cut them up and reassembled the bodies but mixed-up pieces from all the family members. It was like a horror movie. There was blood everywhere. On the walls. The ceiling. The carpet was soaked in it. It was so horrible. People don't realize how bad blood smells when there's a lot of it. I just froze. Don't know how long I stood there before I was able to run outside. I threw up in the flowerbed."

"That must have been terrifying."

I keep my eyes on the table, sure that if I look at Chad I'll burst into tears.

"After that, I thought it would be safest to lock myself in my car while I called 9-1-1."

"I would have done the same thing." His mug rises from the table.

"When I got to my car. There were bloody handprints on both the passenger and driver side windows." I fight to breathe deeply and not hyperventilate.

"You mean... the killer was there the whole time? Watching you go into the house?"

I shudder and nod, then drain my water glass. "The police took my car for a few days to collect evidence. They needed to test the blood." I swallow hard. "The detective showed me a strange line across the palm print and said that there was a good chance that was the killer's blood. When someone is being stabbed, the knife handle gets slippery from all the blood, and the person holding it, well, their hand often slides down the blade and they get cut up." I'm not sure my eggs and toast are going to stay down.

Chad sets his cup on the table. "Did they ever find out who did it?"

"Yes. But they never caught him. The blood on my car belonged to the ex-husband. How could a father do that to his own kids?" I choke back a sob.

Chad leans back in the booth, shaking his head. "Sometimes people just snap."

"I hope they catch him so he can rot in prison until they fry him."

"But it wasn't even *your* family."

Anger flashes over me. "What difference does that make? I still have nightmares every single night. I stayed up for sixty hours last week because I was too afraid to go to sleep. Walking into that house broke me. I don't know how first responders deal with seeing that kind of stuff every day."

Chad sucks his teeth. "I hadn't thought about that. I'm sorry. I can walk you to your car. I don't mind."

I'm not sure I want him to. He seems so blasé about the murders that it freaks me out a little, although it could be that he doesn't understand because he hasn't experienced the true horror of it. "No, I'm good. Thanks."

He raises his hand to flag down the waitress. A hand with a thick scar across the palm.

A Sheet of Glass

By Artemis Greenleaf

"OH, wow!" Maggie dropped her coat on the couch. "This view. It's like a travel brochure."

Rex strolled up to the wall of glass that looked out onto a picture-postcard landscape. A few trees covering the roots of the foothills were bare, but most were spruces and firs. The sunset stained the snow pink where it lay in ragged drifts on Pike's Peak. The regal mountain jutted from the horizon beyond the expansive wooden deck. A bubbling hot tub steamed in the frosty air.

He turned to his wife. "When is your sister getting here again?"

"Saturday. So we have the place to ourselves for a couple of days."

He waggled his eyebrows suggestively.

Maggie joined him by the window, putting her arm around his waist. "I wish Jewel was here to see this."

Rex hugged her shoulders. "It's only two years. She'll be back before you know it."

Maggie sighed. "But Madagascar is so far away. Can't she teach English in the States?"

"I was only getting one bar earlier, so we may have to go into town to get cell service, but we'll have that video call on Christmas Day. She's happy. You'll see. She is her mother's daughter after all."

Maggie disengaged herself from her husband and wandered into the kitchen. "Oh, look. Here's the door to get out onto the deck."

She opened it and Rex followed her outside. A thin layer of snow crunched under their feet as they stepped carefully across the wooden planks. Maggie inhaled deeply, breathing in the scents of ice and evergreens that marked the holiday season for her.

The deck was on the second level of the home, and inaccessible from the ground. Maggie supposed that was partly to deter bears and partly to keep it usable year-round—digging through four feet of snow to get to the hot tub wouldn't be much fun.

She rubbed her arms. "It's too cold out here. I'm going inside."

The couple scurried into the kitchen. Maggie smiled at her husband. "Let's grab the groceries out of the truck. It's a little early to start dinner, but we can at least get unpacked."

After all the bags were emptied and the fire started, Rex went to the kitchen to pour them some wine. Maggie moved around the living room, admiring the eclectic décor. Stone artifacts and wood carvings graced the shelves. A neo-cave painting of running horses, flint arrowheads tucked into cutouts in the sand-colored mat, hung prominently across from the glass wall.

Her lip curled as she approached the fireplace. On either end of the mantel, two ugly carved wooden heads squatted like refugees from a fever dream. As far as Maggie could tell, they represented some kind of animal, but she didn't believe they were living creatures—the closest description she could come up with was if a wolf and an alligator had a baby. Or two.

"Sorry—took me a while to find the corkscrew." Rex handed her a glass, half-filled with shiraz.

She gave him a peck on the cheek before gesturing to the fireplace with her goblet. "Do you think they'll be mad if we put those things in a closet? They give me the creeps, and I'm sure they'll terrify Lizzie's kids."

Rex picked up one of the carvings. "They're hideous, but they're just wood. Maybe turn them to face the wall?"

He set the sculpture down, toothy snout against the paint, then rotated the other to match it.

"My hero!" Maggie took a sip of wine and giggled.

Rex flexed a bicep. "At your service, madame."

He set his glass on the coffee table, and took Maggie's, placing it next to his. Rex wrapped his arms around his wife and kissed her deeply. Dinner forgotten, they made their way to the master bedroom.

Maggie's eyelids popped open, and she listened intently in the dark.

Footsteps.

She shook Rex awake. "I think there's someone in the house."

He propped himself on one elbow. The floor creaked again. He got out of bed, naked, and grabbed a ski pole from the corner. "Stay here."

Through the open door, Maggie could see the change in light as, room by room, lights snapped on throughout the house. After a few minutes, each room in succession went dark.

Footfalls thumped up the stairs.

Maggie clutched the comforter around her throat. "Rex?"

"Yeah. It's me." His familiar figure appeared in the doorway. "There's nobody else in here. All the doors are locked. Starting to snow again. Must be the house settling, or the wind. Not sure. It's alright. I needed to check the fireplace, anyway."

A loud gurgle erupted from Maggie's stomach. "How do you feel about a midnight supper?"

The overnight snow was light and didn't impact their adventures: breakfast and museums in Cripple Creek, lunch aboard the Royal Gorge train, and a little snowshoeing in the afternoon back at the rental.

They were both tired to the bone after a quick-fix dinner and drowsed on the couch with books in their hands. Half-empty wineglasses and plates with a few chocolaty crumbs sat on the coffee table. They hadn't had the energy to mess with the fire tonight. Lamps on the end tables glowed softly on either side of the sofa.

Skreek. Skreek. Skreek.

The noise came again as Maggie drifted up from sleep. She blinked rapidly, as if to squeegee the nightmare apparitions off her eyeballs.

She tried to scream, but her throat constricted and all she could choke out was *Ruh—Ruh—Ruh*. Maggie clutched Rex's arm until her nails dug in, jerking him from slumber.

On the deck, the silhouettes of two creatures with glowing yellow eyes stood peering in at them.

Rex was six feet, and they must have been half again his height. One was slightly taller, and it drew claws across the glass, making the skreeking noise again.

There was nothing between them and the monsters but a picture window. The wall of glass that had revealed the splendid panorama now bared them to the night. There was no hiding from the things outside. They could watch every move Rex and Maggie made, track where they ran to hide.

All with only a sheet of glass less than half an inch thick to protect them.

"Bears... those are bears, right?" Rex moved in front of Maggie. "Do we have bear spray?"

The shorter creature turned its head slightly, as if it were listening to Rex. In profile, its long, thick snout was partly open and sharp teeth glinted in the moonlight.

"Not a bear," Maggie panted.

The loathsome beasts scratched on the glass again, seemingly relishing the terror they created.

"Okay." Rex whispered in Maggie's ear. "We need to get upstairs and lock ourselves in the bedroom. We can move the dresser to barricade the door. On the count of three, run."

Maggie nodded, not sure her legs would work.

"One... two... three!"

Rex vaulted over the back of the couch, but Maggie's legs tangled in the afghan and she nearly fell. He snatched her arm and dragged her to the stairway, then pushed her in front of him. "Go!"

The couple raced up the stairs and slammed the bedroom door closed behind them. Maggie locked it while Rex started pushing the heavy dresser. She joined him and together they heaved the piece into place, blocking the door.

Rex yanked the curtains closed. "What the hell are those things?"

"Don't know. But..."

"But what?" Rex pulled his phone from his pocket.

"You know those carved wooden heads above the fireplace?"

He nodded. "Yeah. Yeah, you're right." He tapped the screen. "Dammit. No service."

"Landline?" Maggie's eyes searched every surface of the room but found no phone.

They pushed the bed against the dresser and locked themselves in the ensuite bathroom, where they shivered in fear, waiting for the sound of shattering glass. The deck creaked and groaned as the creatures paced around most of the night. When the yellow fingers of dawn finally caressed the window, Maggie and Rex unfolded their cramped legs and stiffly got to their feet.

"We have to go into town so I can call my sister and tell her not to come."

Maggie and Rex were shoving their bags into the SUV when a car pulled up. A woman got out and gaped at them.

"Hi. I'm Ellen. With the rental company. Mr. and Mrs. Jackson?"

Rex set a suitcase on the driveway. "Yes, we're the Jacksons. We can't stay here any longer. Sorry."

"Oh? What seems to be the problem? I'm sure we can rem—"

"No, I don't think you can. We were attacked last night." Maggie hugged herself.

"Attacked? What happened? Did you call the police?"

"Come on. We'll show you." Rex turned and re-entered the house, Maggie and Ellen trailing behind him.

Rex walked straight to the wall of glass. Thick clouds glowered over the forest, swallowing the tops of the foothills. "Out here. Last night. We were sitting on the couch and these things were on the deck, looking in at us and scratching the glass."

Ellen moved to stand next to him. She looked out onto the deck and frowned. "What things? The deck is covered in snow from yesterday afternoon. There aren't any footprints..."

"That's impossible!" Maggie ran and put her hands on the glass. "They were standing right here. We both saw them. They paced back and forth on the deck all night."

"Can you describe the creatures?"

Maggie chewed the inside of her cheek. "You already think we're crazy."

"Of course I don't. Just tell me what you saw."

Maggie and Rex shared a long look.

"They were tall." Rex looked up at the glass, then pointed to the HVAC duct on an adjacent wall. "They were about the same height as that. Nine, ten feet. At first, I thought they might be bears, but they had glowing yellow eyes and long snouts, like an alligator."

Maggie shrieked.

Both Ellen's and Rex's heads whipped around toward her. Maggie threw herself into Rex's arms. "Did you…? Did you turn those horrible things back around?"

"What?" Rex slid an arm around her waist.

"Those heads! The ones we turned to face the wall when we got here? They look just like the creatures on the deck!"

Ellen followed Maggie's gaze to the mantle. Two monstrous carved wood heads grinned menacingly at her. She walked over to the fireplace and picked one up, then shook her head.

"I'm really sorry. Gilbert—our office manager—collects… unusual things. He tends to leave them in the rental properties instead of putting them in his own house, because sometimes they have entities attached to them." She picked up the other head. "I'll just take these away with me so that Aponi Dosela can cleanse them. She's our local shaman."

"Entities?" Maggie squeaked. "What do you mean by entities?"

Ellen looked from one grotesque head to the other. "Like spirits. Ghosts."

"You're trying to tell me that we were haunted by ghost…" Rex waved his hand toward the carvings. "Whatever those are? Ghosts? Are you serious?"

"That would explain the lack of footprints. I'll come back and smudge the house later, but they shouldn't bother you anymore."

Rex pulled Maggie closer. "You can do what you want. We're leaving."

"I'm sorry. You can't do that."

"I don't care about the deposit. We're going to go find a hotel."

"I'm not talking about the deposit, Mr. Jackson. I came up here to make sure you had food. There's a storm coming in and you won't be able to get off the mountain. Roads out of town are already closed."

A breeze swirled through the snow that lay on the deck.

Ellen held one head in each hand. "I've got to get to my own home now. Do not be foolish enough to attempt to drive in white-out conditions. You'll be perfectly safe here. I have some things for you."

Maggie glanced over her shoulder to the sheet of glass. "Are you sure? I don't think I could take another night with those things outside."

"I'm certain of it. No one has ever reported seeing anything like that before. Gilbert visited a traveling antiques auction over the weekend. Tried to get me to go with him—maybe I should have, to keep him out of trouble. These were not here when the last guests checked out on Monday."

Maggie sighed and bit her lip. Then she and Rex followed Ellen out to the cars. She opened the back passenger door and pulled out two shopping bags. "I didn't know what you had, so I made sure you had some bare necessities."

Rex took the bags and sighed. "Thank you."

"Call me if you need anything." A snowflake fell onto Ellen's dark jacket. And then another. "Stay inside until the storm blows over. It may take the plow a while to get this far out to clear the road."

Maggie and Rex watched as she drove away with the horrible heads. He took the shopping that Ellen had given them, while she picked up a couple of their hastily packed bags from the back of the SUV and trudged inside.

Back in the living room, Maggie stared out the wall of glass as the sky sifted silent snowflakes like powdered sugar over the trees.

"It feels like we're in a reverse snow globe."

Rex pulled a pack of batteries out of the shopping bag and moved to stand next to his wife.

She leaned against him. "Do you think ghosts are real?"

"There is more gravy than grave about you."

"Humbug!" She turned his chin so he faced her. "Old Jacob Marley, tell me more. Speak comfort to me, Jacob!"

Rex chuckled. "In the cold light of day, what I think happened is that we accidentally bought the wrong kind of brownies or something while we were shopping. We saw those hideous carvings, and the THC did the rest."

"Seems weird we'd both see and hear the same things."

He shrugged. "As Ellen pointed out, there were no footprints. If those… things had been physical animals, there would have been prints galore."

Maggie bit her lip and pulled away from him.

"Where you going?"

"I noticed some duct tape in the utility room. I'm going to check for extra sheets in the back bedroom. I've got to cover that glass before nightfall."

BAGMAN

By Holly Dey

"COUSIN Useless!" Eustace hadn't heard that in ages, but he'd never outgrown the nickname.

"Daisy! You're not a child anymore." Rose Donovan elbowed her younger daughter away from the front door. "Sorry about that. Come in, Eustace." She paused when her eyes fell on the man standing behind her nephew on the front porch.

With a megawatt grin that would put a politician to shame, the stranger reached out his hand. "Charisma Cooper." He winked at her. "I bet you thought ole Eustace here was bringin' a lady friend."

"I did. Won't you come in?"

Aunt Rose's home was just like Eustace remembered from way back when. Although it seemed much smaller than when he was a kid.

"Thank you, ma'am. Don't think nothin' of it—happens every day."

"Let me introduce you around. You've met Eustace's cousin, Daisy. Her boys, Tyson and Zachary are out feedin' the cows. They'll be along after while. His other cousins are Rocky...."

Rocky Donovan raised his hand. "Hiya."

"Rocky's daughter, Hope...."

A pretty blonde smiled at the newcomers.

"Her mama, Darla, is on the way. She'll be here in a little bit."

"Primrose...." A middle-aged woman with short salt-and-pepper hair nodded. "Most people call me PC."

"Sittin' next to her is her good friend, Drew." The man was holding a small beige dog, who didn't growl, but bared his teeth at Eustace and Charisma. "Hello. Nice to meet you." He stroked the dog's head. "Easy Cordite. It's okay."

Rose put her arm around the man standing next to her, who wore an outlandish Christmas-themed Hawaiian shirt. "This is my best friend and neighbor, Terry."

Charisma grinned again. "It's real nice to meet all y'all."

Eustace sighed. He knew Charisma would remember every little thing about each and every one of the people in the room. Eustace could barely remember who was who, and most of them were his kinfolks.

"Thanks for invitin' us to Christmas Eve dinner, Aunt Rose." Eustace hadn't seen his cousins in… well, he couldn't actually remember, it had been so long. It was before his father's brother, Uncle Trey, was gunned down in a convenience store robbery. Aunt Rose always sent him a Christmas letter, whenever she was able to find him.

Trouble seemed to dog Eustace's steps like a starving hound looking for scraps. He wasn't a violent man—he never hurt anybody. Not physically, anyway. But he couldn't seem to stay out of jail for more than a year or two at a time. He'd met Charisma at a halfway house. No idea why the man had taken a shine to him. Butter wouldn't melt in his mouth, and there didn't seem to be any reason he'd need to hang around useless Eustace.

"You still with the po-lice, Prim—PC?" Eustace smiled at his cousin.

"Technically, I'm retired, but I do some contract work for the Possumwood PD."

Eustace only asked because he wanted Charisma to be on his best behavior and not get any ideas. Was it too much to ask to just enjoy one holiday with his family?

The glowing Christmas tree at the far end of the spacious living room caught Eustace's eye, and he moved closer to it. White lights shone among the branches of the artificial Douglas fir and vintage glass ornaments, as well as ones that were clearly made by two generations of children, dangled from the limbs. There were too many presents to fit under the boughs, and cheerful stacks of gifts rose all around the festive evergreen.

But what really caught Eustace's eye was the angel on top of the tree. Her hands and face were porcelain. Metallic gold wings rose majestically behind her red brocaded dress. A thick green belt was topped with a luminous red jewel and gold cording.

Thing was, Eustace could not escape the feeling that she was looking at him. Him, specifically, out of all the people in the room. And she was not happy.

"She's gorgeous, ain't she?"

Eustace hadn't heard Daisy coming up to his side.

"Yeah."

"Mama got her at Vintage Glory Antiques, downtown. S'posed to be from the 1800s."

"How 'bout that."

"You hungry? Mama made her famous divinity candy. There's a few other lil snacks to tide us over while we're waitin' on Darla and the boys."

Eustace nodded and let Daisy lead him to the small counter underneath a window between the living room and the kitchen. It was a handy place for party snacks, and it reminded him of a fast-food drive through. Only without the glass and cashier.

A plate of white fudge.

A serving dish of colorful kebabs—a toothpick stuck through a green grape, topped with a banana slice, topped with a strawberry, topped with a mini marshmallow.

Cheese and crackers.

Texas trash snack mix.

Whatever had been cooking in the kitchen for dinner smelled so good it nearly brought a tear to his eye. His meals and accommodations since leaving the halfway house had been... bare bones budget. Eustace was almost to the point where he'd rather go hungry than eat another peanut butter cracker. And here were these beautiful morsels spread before him, with the promise of a decadent holiday meal in just a little while.

He picked up a piece of divinity and popped the whole piece into his mouth. As he turned around, the silky sweet fudge spreading over his tongue, Eustace was in heaven. Until he noticed Charisma standing next to Hope. Rocky must have had the same thought, because he was wedging himself between the two of them.

Soon enough, Darla strolled through the front door, and not even Charisma's charm was enough to keep Hope away from her mother. Daisy's two strapping sons came in, and dinner was served. Eustace couldn't help himself—he went back for seconds and then thirds. But he still managed to squeeze in some pie, both cherry and pecan.

Rose herded everyone into the living room to play a pass-the-parcel game. Eustace made sure to sit in front of the tree, his back to the angel. He was ashamed to look her in the face. At the end of the game, each player was left with an absurd present. Eustace got a dirt-scented candle and Charisma ended up with a box of macaroni-and-cheese-flavored candy canes.

"Oh!" Rose looked at her watch. "It's after 11:30. We need to load up if we're going to get to the Christmas Eve service by midnight."

Charisma yawned. "Ms. Donovan? Eustace and I had a real long bus ride to get here this afternoon. Can't speak for him, but I'm tired to the bone, and I sure would be embarrassed to fall asleep in church."

Eustace's shoulders drooped. Not because he didn't want to miss a midnight church service, but because he knew Charisma was up to something. The con had quizzed him about his family during the entire trip.

"Of course, honey. Rocky, would you get that cot out of my room right quick?" She turned back to Charisma. "If you open up the ottoman, there's some afghans and fleece throws in there."

"Thank you so much, ma'am."

The moment they were alone in the house, Charisma rubbed his hands together. "We hit the jackpot! How we gonna get all this stuff outta here?"

"You want to rob my family while they're at church?"

Charisma laughed. "It ain't like you ever see 'em." Then his eyes darkened and his lips became a thin line. "You seem to forget I own you, boy. If it wasn't for me, that narco woulda left your carcass to rot in a field. It's because of me that you ain't in a homeless camp and you get to eat every day."

Eustace sighed and looked up at the angel. *I wish it didn't have to be like this.* A tear welled in his eye as he shambled into the kitchen to look for trash bags.

Charisma was an experienced burglar. He filled three leaf and lawn bags with valuables, and more than a few Christmas packages, in record time. Eustace worked at a much slower pace, racking his brain for a way to get out of his predicament. To get away from Charisma. But as usual, he came up empty.

"Come on! That's good enough. They'll be back soon."

Eustace carried his half-empty bag and picked up another that Charisma had stuffed full to bursting. But when they got to where they expected the door to be, there was just a smooth, blank wall.

Charisma whipped his head one way, then the other. "Where's the damn door?" He set his ill-gotten gains on the floor and felt along the wall with both hands. "It's gotta be here somewhere!"

But it was not.

They searched and then felt every wall in every room with an exterior wall in the house, except for PC's room. Cordite was shut in there, and neither man wanted to risk the bite that he threatened behind the door.

There was not an exit to be found.

The church service must surely be over by now. In a panic, Charisma picked up a wooden chair from the kitchen and tried to break a window.

The chair bounced off the glass and hit him in the face, breaking his nose. He swore a blue streak as blood flowed freely onto his shirt.

Eustace brought him a roll of paper towels. "I think—"

"No you don't."

"I think we should put everything back."

"What?"

"You can't rob somebody's house on Christmas Eve. That's just...."

Charisma laughed, blowing bubbles of blood through his nose. "You tink dey hab sub kide ob superdatural scurity systeb?"

"Okay. Then you explain just where the heck the doors are?"

Charisma glowered. Eustace returned to the living room and began putting the purloined presents back under the tree, smiling when he noticed a tag with his name on it. Grudgingly, Charisma directed Eustace to where he'd taken the other items so they, too, could be replaced.

The bags were empty, but no doors appeared.

"Got adny bore bright itheas?" Charisma grumbled. He waved one of the sacks around, then stopped and peered inside. "What's this?"

Eustace moved closer to take the final item and put it away.

Charisma reached into the bag. And was jerked inside with a startled yelp.

"Hey!" Eustace lifted the now empty trash bag from the floor. He didn't see hide nor hair of his companion. His pulse raced. Was he next? Eustace dropped the sack like it was lava. "Charisma?" His breath was so fast and shallow the name stuck in his teeth.

There was no reply.

Voices came from the front porch. Eustace snatched up the plastic sacks and shoved them under the couch. The front door opened, and his relatives and their friends spilled in.

"We didn't wake you, did we, Eustace?" Rose smiled at him.

"No. I was still up."

PC scanned the room. "Where's Charisma?"

"Oh, he had to go." Eustace glanced at the angel and felt sure she was smiling this time. "Guess Christmas just ain't his bag."

SIREN SONG

By A. B. Richards

IGROANED as my 4 AM alarm jangled. *Why? Why did I promise my sister that I'd go Black Friday shopping with her?* I sighed and peeled the covers off.

"Wake up, Shopaholic." I elbowed Janine.

She and her daughter had spent the night, since they were over for Thanksgiving, anyway. Chelsea had the guest room, but my sister and I had stayed up talking until 2:30 and slept on the pull-out in the living room.

I crept upstairs to brush my teeth and get dressed, hoping not to wake my husband. Jeff was an early riser, but not this early. I was sorely tempted to slip under the covers, snuggle against his warm body, and go back to sleep.

But a promise is a promise.

When I got back downstairs, Janine and Chelsea were in the kitchen. The coffee pot was gurgling and the aroma of toast wafted across the room to tease my stomach. I rarely ate breakfast, but today would be an exception. I needed all the help I could get staying awake.

A light tapping came from the front door. Janine and I looked at each other.

"Mom," we said in unison.

I let her in while Janine stirred the scrambled eggs.

My mother stood in the doorway dressed in a hot pink tracksuit and sneakers. She looked more like she was ready for a marathon than shopping. Unfortunately for me, that's probably exactly what she had in mind—a shopping marathon. Mom never missed the Black Friday sales. Janine had inherited the shopping gene from her, but it had skipped me. I didn't care for it, not even a little, and that went triple for the designated day of holiday mayhem that was Black Friday. One glass too many of Thanksgiving wine had sealed my fate.

Unless I could find a loophole.

Mom and Janine hugged. Chelsea, whose head rested on the table next to her cereal bowl, gave her a half-hearted wave. Her bright blue unicorn tee-shirt was more lively than she was.

"Hey, Janine? She looks so tired, poor thing. Mom's got her shopping shoes on, so if you want, I can stay here with Chelsea. That way she doesn't slow you down, and she doesn't get exhausted. Safe to say, Mom's shopping extravaganzas can be a bit much for anybody, much less an eight-year-old."

"That's so sweet of you to offer to sacrifice your shopping trip! But Farley's Department Store is offering a free Twigby doll to the first 100 customers. Chelsea is hoping for a Froebel—they're very hard to come by."

"If you know the kind she wants…"

Janine's eyes fell lovingly on her sleepy daughter. "You'll understand when you have kids, Sami. She wants to pick it out herself."

Of course she does. I couldn't even beg my husband to pretend to be sick enough that I needed to stay home and take care of him, because he always played golf on Black Friday with his dad and two brothers. Always. He could fall and have a bone sticking out of his thigh and he'd still go. *Looks like I'm going to have to rustle up some coupons.*

I forced my lips into a smile and scooped eggs and toast on a plate, finding my chair via the coffee maker.

As it turned out, Chelsea was the proud bearer of ticket number 98. Christmas Muzak washing over us, she skipped up to the woman dressed as Mrs. Claus and handed her the electric lime slip of paper. She put it in a bucket and allowed my niece access to the white-picket-fenced area behind her that contained a splendid gold and red velvet sofa, a Christmas tree, and piles of presents.

"Froebel!" Chelsea squealed.

As she exited the gate, doll box hugged tightly against her chest, Mrs. Claus handed her a piece of paper. "Don't forget to come see Santa and get your picture taken! He'll be here in another hour. "

Chelsea nodded as she took the order form. Janine cleared her throat.

"Thank youuuuuuu!" The little girl dragged the 'u' behind her all the way to where we stood.

Janine smiled and waved, but Mrs. Claus was already on to number 99.

"Nana, look! It's Froebel! I got a Froebel."

Mom leaned over to examine the packaged doll. Two boisterous boys raced by and one of them clipped Mom's hip as he passed, nearly flattening her.

"Hey!" I shouted after them.

They continued running at top speed.

Janine sighed. "You okay, Mom?"

"I'm fine, sweetie." Mom looked at Froebel and ran her hand over one of Chelsea's pigtails. "You know, it's a little hectic in here. It might be best for Froebel if your Aunt Sami puts her in the trunk of the car, so she doesn't get upset by all the ruckus."

Chelsea's eyes got wide, and she clutched the box. "Nana? She's not alive. You know that, right?"

Janine scrubbed a hand down her face and Mom grinned. "Yes, my precious one. I know that. I just don't want anything to happen to her, what with these rowdy kids running amok."

"What's a muck?"

"It's a wild animal from the mountains—"

"Mother!" Janine huffed.

I shook my head. "Nana's just teasing. Running amok means being wild and crazy."

Chelsea bit her lip and looked at the box. "I just got Froebel and I don't want her to get broken." Another group of children nearly knocked over a clearance rack. "Would you please put her in the car, Aunt Sami?"

"Of course." I took the doll and headed for the exit. Perhaps I'd be able to linger for a bit and watch the sunrise.

When I came back in, I sat on a bench near the front door to tie my shoe. Two men stood out like volcano zits on picture day. They wore dark suits and clearly had earpieces. Like three-letter secret agents. One was blond and the other a redhead. The blond held up a device about a third the size of a mobile phone, and then they talked to each other, and presumably to whoever was on the other side of the earpieces.

My blood ran cold. Was the government worried something was going to happen? A terrorist attack? A crazy gunman? Organized thieves? I should grab my family and get out of here. Plenty of other stores for Mom and Janine to shop 'til they dropped. I hurried down the aisles, looking for them.

A flash of potent pink disappeared behind a shelf of sheets. I hurried to head her off at the pass, slipping through a row of towels and bathmats.

The person in pink was not my mother. I paused next to the shower curtain rods to reconnoiter. No sign of the fam in housewares. Mom always has a strategy. The last time I went shopping with her during a big sale, she started on the second floor—clothing, makeup, perfume—and worked her way down to the literal bargain basement. I elbowed my way through the obstinate crowd to the up escalator.

Winding my way through the labyrinth of women's clothing, I thought I spotted Chelsea in Men's Shoes, but it was just a little girl wearing the same shirt. She suddenly ran off after another child, whom I assumed was a friend or sibling and they were doing their best to find their own amusement in this orgy of consumerism.

Maybe Mom and Janine started with the basement this year? I struggled to the down escalator and took it all the way to the bitter end.

The basement wasn't nearly as crowded as the other two floors. The tinny Christmas music barely came through down here. And there was Janine, picking through discontinued Correlle dinnerware patterns. Mom was a few shelves over, evaluating skillets.

"There you are!" I looked around. "Where's Chelsea?"

Janine turned her head. "She's right—" She took in a sharp breath. "Chelse? Chelsea, where are you?"

There was no reply. Even Mom looked up and scanned the area. There was no answer to Janine's question. We all spread out and began calling for her. There was not a hint of her sky-blue shirt. Janine became more and more frantic.

I put my hand on her arm. "Don't panic. There's tons of kids running around like lunatics in the store. She probably just started playing with some of them. You go to customer service and tell them she's missing, and Mom and I will keep looking for her."

Janine nodded and ran to the escalator.

I pointed to the right. "Okay, Mom. You go that way. I'll go this way, and we can meet in the middle."

The layout of the upper floors was essentially a big figure eight, and I assumed as above, so below.

"Chelsea!" I called to my niece. There was no natural light in the basement, and as I crept further into the bowels of the building, the sallow florescent lights buzzed and flickered. Clearance racks thinned and disappeared, and the open area gradually tapered into a tunnel. The light dimmed with every step as the bulbs were spaced farther and farther apart, and only about half were working.

Near the escalator, my niece's name had echoed, bouncing off concrete floors and pinging off steel columns. Now, when I shouted her name, the walls swallowed my words. There were doors every few yards on alternate sides of the corridor. I tried every one of them, but none would open.

"Mom? Chelsea?" Silence.

The music started getting louder and more robust. I hoped that meant I was passing through the maintenance area and back into the customer zone.

Voices. Children's voices. Up ahead, one of the doors was about halfway open. *Please, please, please let Chelsea be in there.* I stepped inside. There must have been twenty kids running around. Another dozen stood quietly by the far wall.

A tsunami of relief poured over me when I spotted Chelsea playing with another little girl. I started in that direction and was about to call out to her when the other girl suddenly stopped the game they were playing and walked quickly to the center of the room. There was something that looked like the unholy union of a massage table and a dentist's chair. It was a padded, clinical exam seat, but it had a large hole below the headrest.

The girl sat down, and the contraption reclined. Three sets of tentacles squirmed out from the sides and wrapped around the girl, one set around her chest, one around her waist, and the last around the tops of her thighs. I gasped and tried to convince myself that it was some leftover Halloween prop. That it was just a silly game. The child didn't seem remotely afraid of the pulsating restraints, after all.

"Chelsea! Come on, it's time to go."

Silence blanketed the room. Every last eyeball turned to me.

"Sorry. Not trying to spoil your fun. I just need my niece. Carry on."

With one weird voice, they all shouted, "Get her!"

My flight instinct kicked in and I scrambled out of the room, slamming the door shut behind me, knowing that would buy me only a couple of seconds. I raced down the darkened tunnel as the mob of kids boiled out of the room and pelted after me.

Up ahead, the tunnel dead ended into another corridor. *Right or left? Right or left?* I started left, then veered right at the last second, unsure why I changed my mind.

I could hardly hear anything above my ragged breathing. Except the Christmas music. The clear and perfect Christmas music that seemed to invite me to slow down and enjoy the lovely party that the children were eager to have with me. I slowed my pace. *They would catch up with me in a moment. I should just wait for them.*

A door to my right opened. I barely had time to turn my head before a hand grabbed my arm and jerked me inside, slamming and locking the door behind me.

"Hey!"

Another hand covered my mouth and a voice hissed in my ear. "Shhhhh! Not a word."

I struggled as foam plugs were stuffed into my ears. "What do you think—"

The red-haired agent I'd seen earlier by the front door raised his index finger to his lips. I swallowed and shook my head. I didn't want to play with the kids anymore, just grab my niece and get the hell outta Dodge.

The agent clasped my wrist and started away from the door. We were in yet another tunnel, this one smaller and mostly occupied by large pipes. I assumed it was an access corridor for plumbing or HVAC.

I hesitated. "I have to get Chelsea."

He shook his head and continued pulling on my arm. "Not yet."

I read his lips more than heard his words. These earplugs were good.

I knew he was right. If I stepped into that mob of kids, bad things would happen. But it didn't make me feel any better about leaving my niece in the thick of it. Telling myself that my sudden and untimely demise would not get her home safely, I followed the agent.

We jogged alongside pipes that were taller than me. Smaller tubes were bracketed to both the top and bottom. From time to time, a sinister groaning reverberated in the large pipe, causing the smaller ones to shudder. I couldn't so much hear it as feel it in my bones. With each tremble, the agent picked up the pace.

A stitch burned in my side and my legs quivered. Just when I didn't think I could take another step, the agent stopped. I leaned over, hands on my thighs, gasping for breaths that laced fire along my ribs.

The agent began spinning what appeared to be a steering wheel on top of a hatch that protruded out of the floor about two feet.

One of my earplugs slipped out and I heard frantic pounding from the inside of the metal door. I tried, with little success, to slow my loud panting to silent breathing.

The hatch flew open and the red-haired agent reached in and dragged the blond one out, the hatch door clanging shut the moment his feet cleared the shaft. The second agent was dripping wet and carried a grey box a little larger than a pack of cards. Agent Yellow clutched his side and fell over. Bright blood blossomed on his torn white shirt, spreading quickly up the wet fabric.

Agent Red took the box and set it aside before yanking the tattered shirttail up and out of the way. The wound was the size of a large dinner plate, an angry red ring with a bleeding hole at the center.

I froze. I had never seen anything like it and had no idea what to do. Agent Red pulled something from his breast pocket and tore the wrapper off, wiping as much blood as he could with a gauze square before slapping what looked like an over-sized Band-Aid on the wound.

Even now I could not tell you what possessed me to walk over to the hatch and lift the cover. I don't know what I expected to see, but I was not at all prepared for what was in the bottom of the access shaft.

An eye.

An eye that was bigger around than the tube. An eye where nebulas floated and a galaxy's worth of stars shimmered around a black hole at the center. As I stared into the abyss, the music started. It was what I imagined a chorus of angels would sound like, and I could not look away. It was the most beautiful thing I'd ever seen. And heard.

Something slammed into my left side, knocking me to the floor. As I rolled onto my back, Agent Red slammed the hatch door and cranked the wheel. About a foot of slimy olive-green tentacle clung to my wrist, frantically wriggling, as he tightened the wheel and severed it. There was a horrific screech that I thought would shred my brain, and I clapped my hands to my ears.

The silence that followed hurt, like a blade being pulled from a wound. I curled into a fetal position on the floor, rubbing the sore spot just below the palm of my hand. Blood trickled from a small wound at the center of a red circle.

Agent Red pulled out his earplugs and shook his head.

I jumped as something cold and wet slid across my forearm. Red leaned over and grabbed the writhing piece of tentacle that had started climbing up my arm. Holding it at arm's length, he pulled out a small glass bottle from another pocket in his jacket. He dropped the tentacle and poured a sulfur yellow powder on it. The thing contorted and squirmed as it dried out and began to collapse in on itself.

"What is that?" I swallowed hard.

"Dust, now." He ground the last few chunks into powder with the heel of his shoe. "Can't leave any live pieces. They regrow."

"Into what?" I didn't like how much my voice quavered.

"We call it The Songbird. But you can think of it as a giant alien squid that's learned how to control people with subliminal messages."

Agent Red picked up the grey box and helped Agent Yellow to his feet.

I got up as well. "That makes no sense."

Red shrugged, then pulled Agent Yellow's arm across his shoulder. "Lot of things don't."

"What does it want? What was it doing with those children?" *What was it going to do to Chelsea?*

"It feeds off energy. The kids it got to will be okay in a week or two. They will have to be monitored, though. Once it got its literal hooks into them, they'll always be more vulnerable to it."

"I still don't understand why they were all down there. I mean…"

"It influenced someone in the office to make a recording of it and play it along with the holiday music throughout the store. You looked into its eye. Saw for yourself how persuasive it can be. You never even noticed the arm coming up the shaft for you."

He wasn't wrong. "The recording… is what's in the grey box?"

"Yes."

The concrete floor slanted upward, and it wasn't long before we came to a freight dock. A blue van with an anthropomorphic cartoon plunger decal was parked nearby. White block letters read 'PLUMBERS' across the side.

As we approached, the back doors opened and two men in white coveralls jumped out and pulled a stretcher from inside the van. They loaded Agent Yellow onto it and whisked him inside.

"Aren't you afraid I'll tell someone about this?"

Agent Red paused before he climbed into the back of the van. "Go ahead. Tell anybody you want. See what happens." He laughed, got into the vehicle, and slammed the doors behind him. Tires screeched as the driver punched the accelerator, and I found myself all alone in the loading dock, with no idea how to get back inside the store.

I'm sure it seemed a lot longer than it actually took to find a gate and walk all the way around the outside of the store to an entrance. My mind was still reeling from what had just happened. Did I really see what I just saw? That couldn't have happened. Could it? My brain felt like it was about to short circuit and exhaustion from all the fleeing was creeping up my legs.

I sat on a bench just inside the front door to tie my shoe. Maybe I could rest for a minute before I entered the spend-fest and started the searching expedition for my family.

"Aunt Sami! Wake up, silly!" I jumped as Chelsea shook my shoulder.

Mom chuckled. "We just sent you out to put Froebel in the car. Never dreamed you'd stop for a nap on the way back."

Janine set two oversized shopping bags on the floor.

Had I dreamed the whole thing? Now that was something that made sense. Of course, the whole subliminal squid thing was just some crazy dream.

I felt so much better as I stood up. The world had shifted from crazy to kilter in seconds. Sure, I felt a little dumb for falling asleep on a bench at the mall, but that was so much better than the alternative.

Janine picked up the shopping. "What have you done to yourself, Sami?" She pointed to my wrist.

I stared down at a round, red weal, about the size of a fifty-cent piece, dried blood crusted over a small wound at the center.

Blunt Force Trauma

By Holly Dey

"Don't even think of bringing banana bread." Laura Reinhart wagged a finger. "I *always* bring banana bread."

Amity Hudson was leaning back in the plastic chair as far as she dared, lazily ruffling eighty-pound Jax's ears as he rested his head on her thigh. Her other dog, Amber, snored in the corner, next to her barn buddies Teddy and Mudflap.

"Salad or dessert?" Jackie Barber tapped a clipboard on her desk.

"What if I split the difference and bring a fruit salad?"

"Works for me." Jackie scribbled some notes. "Alright. Go get tacked up. I've got another lesson after you. You know how Thursdays are."

Amity hummed Christmas songs under her breath as she went to the tack room to get her saddle and bridle. The red and white felt stockings tacked on the stall doors, each horse's name written in glitter glue on the white cuff, made her smile. The barn Christmas party was her favorite of all the holiday events. Her black Irish Sport Horse mare, Destiny, was already in her stall, groomed and ready to go.

As Amity neared the tack room door, a muffled female voice purred from somewhere inside. Assuming it was just other riders talking, Amity walked right in.

Simon Edgemont stood near his saddle rack. Diana McMurphy, the newly hired assistant trainer, stood close to him. Way too close.

Amity cleared her throat. Simon cast his guilty eyes to the cement floor. Diana smirked as she walked toward Amity, then out the door.

"Planning on going for a ride?" Amity asked, her voice clipped.

He mumbled something and grabbed his saddle, rushing past without looking at her. Amity clenched her jaw. Simon was her best friend's husband. Amity hadn't caught him and Diana doing anything other than talking, granted in a far too intimate way. But the way Simon had reacted to her seeing them together...

She didn't want to break Kathy's heart by telling her the love of her life might be straying, but if Amity was married and her spouse was getting frisky with someone else, she'd want to know. Maybe an affair could be nipped in the bud with an earnest conversation.

Amity picked up her jumping bridle and saddle, trying to decide what to do as she carried them to Destiny's stall.

After she tacked up the mare and Amity was leading her down the aisleway to the arena, she noticed Diana in the stall with one of the teen riders, Kymberleigh Fields. Her horse, Flyboy, was green and needed mileage. Every time Kym went to a show and didn't do nearly as well as she'd hoped, Jackie reminded her of that. They'd been to a big show this past weekend, and yet again, Flyboy finished out of the ribbons. In all honesty, he was too much horse for Kym, but her mother was crazy about the big chestnut, and wouldn't dream of selling him on.

Jax had growled at Diana the first time he'd seen her. Amity was inclined to trust his assessment. She'd read somewhere that animals with one blue eye see the spirit world with it, so maybe he could see good and evil, too. Not sure she entirely believed that, but he was highly sensitive.

Amber, on the other hand, was a silent guardian, neither barking nor snarling, just putting her large black body between Amity and the threat and staring. The tan markings above her eyes tended to make her look angry, even when she was happy.

Amber often stared at Diana.

Once Amity was on Destiny's back, all thoughts of Diana faded away. It was a good lesson, and her legs were wobbly from the work without stirrups by the end. It was a little too chilly to hose Destiny off, so Amity walked her with a wool cooler on until she was ready to be put away.

As she led Destiny around, she noticed Simon riding in the outside jumping arena. Diana leaned against the fence. Normally, Simon just trail rode, but it was dark already. Nothing wrong with trail riding—at least he had some interest in horses. He and Kathy often came out to the barn together, where Simon and Daryl, his buckskin gelding, would stroll around the pasture while Kathy took a lesson.

Amity's gut clenched. She'd thought those two were the perfect couple. Now she wasn't so sure. She waffled back and forth about whether to call her friend. Should she talk to Simon first, get his side of the story? If he was cheating, though, he'd certainly lie. With a heavy heart, she decided to make the worst call of her life on the way home.

She put Destiny away and gave her some cookies. On the way to her car, Amity noticed Jackie and Diana arguing in the barn aisle. She changed directions, but Laura came out of the office and broke up the disagreement.

Relieved, Amity got in her car. Once she was on a straight stretch of road, she made the call.

"Hey girl, what's up?" Kathy's voice was cheerful, and Amity heard glasses clinking in the background.

"Hey." She couldn't just spit her bad news out without preamble. "Where are you? Sounds like a restaurant."

Kathy chuckled. "I wish. Loading the dishwasher."

It was time to rip the bandage off. "Is Simon there with you?"

"No… He went to go watch the game with some friends. Why do you ask?"

"I'm sure I saw him out here. Riding…"

Kathy was silent for so long that Amity thought the call had dropped. "Hello? Kathy?"

"I'm here. Look, I have to go." She hung up.

Amity wiped moisture from her eye. *That went well. Not.*

The fruit seemed less colorful than normal as Amity chopped strawberries and mangoes. She threw them into a large bowl and added grapes and blueberries. Her Secret Santa gift sat on the table near her purse so she wouldn't forget to take it.

She'd lost her appetite for the Christmas party, but she'd promised the fruit salad and signed up for the gift exchange. Amity had called Kathy several times on Friday, but her friend hadn't picked up. *Probably hates me now.*

Amity usually rode on Saturday mornings, and had planned to do so before the party, hoping it would make her feel better. With a sigh, she stretched plastic wrap over the bowl and called the dogs.

Bright lights danced around the parking lot. Problem was, they weren't the Christmas kind. They were the red and blue kind. An icy fist grabbed her innards. *What happened? Is someone hurt? Is Destiny okay?*

A police officer stopped her as she turned into the driveway.

"I'm sorry, ma'am. No visitors today."

"I have to check on my horse! What's going on?"

"Do you know Diana McMurphy?"

What's that cow done now? "Yes."

"Detectives probably want to talk to you, then. You can park over there." He pointed to the horse trailers. "And please leave your dogs in the car. It's in the fifties. They should be fine with the windows cracked."

Amity nodded and parked her SUV, rolling down each window a few inches. She half-jogged over to the barn, where yellow crime scene tape billowed in the breeze. Jackie sat on a tack trunk across from Flyboy's stall.

"What happened?" Amity sat next to her.

"What a day." Jackie rubbed her forehead. "So, when the boys came to feed this morning, Flyboy's stall door was open, and he was gone. They called me, thought he'd been stolen. I came running out of the house and saw him grazing by the outdoor dressage arena. Halter and lead rope were still on him. Which was a little strange, but everything seemed to be fine. You know how he unties knots? I just assumed he'd figured out how to open stall doors now." She sniffled. "But then he had the halter on. That scared me, because what if someone really had tried to steal him, and something scared them off?"

"If Flyboy wasn't stolen, then why are the police here?"

"I took him back to his stall, and—" She swallowed hard and closed her eyes for a moment. "I found her. Diana."

"What was she doing in Flyboy's stall?" Amity recalled the assistant trainer talking to Kym on Thursday night.

"She was dead. Somebody hit her in the face… there was a steel pipe in the stall. They must have used that. It was awful."

Amity put her arm around her coach. "Oh, Jackie. I'm so sorry. You got the person on camera, right?"

"That's the thing. Somebody pulled the main switch and shut off the power. People do it accidentally all the time when they turn on the lights for the outdoor arena. That's what I get for using a discount electrician. The backup batteries in the cameras were dead."

How convenient.

A man with an athletic build in a sport coat came out of the stall and stopped in front of Jackie and Amity.

"Ms. Barber." He addressed Jackie, then looked pointedly at Amity.

"It's okay, Detective Myles. She can hear what you have to say."

"It looks like Ms. McMurphy surprised the thief. We'll know more after the autopsy. You might want to do something different with your fuse box to limit access to the main breaker. It's a real shame you have cameras, but they were all off." His gaze turned to Amity. "Do you own a horse here?"

Amity nodded and looked down the aisle to Destiny, who nickered, no doubt wondering where her cookies were.

"Did you know Diana McMurphy?"

"Yes."

"Would you mind coming with me? I'd like to ask you a few questions."

Amity got up. She did mind. The woman that her best friend's husband was possibly having an affair with had been murdered. And she'd been the one to spill the tea. She didn't want to lie to the cops, but she didn't want to throw her friend under the bus, either. Although it was true she hadn't mentioned Diana by name, only told Kathy that Simon was at the barn when he was supposed to be somewhere else.

The detective led her into the office. He sat behind Jackie's desk and Amity sat in a plastic chair. He pulled out a notepad and a pen, then took her name and contact information.

"Ms. Hudson. When was the last time you saw Ms. McMurphy?"

"Thursday night."

"And what was she doing?"

"I… saw her talking to Simon Edgemont." *And arguing with Jackie. Crap.* "When I left, she was in a discussion with Jackie and Laura. That's Laura Rienhart. She boards here, too."

"Did you hear what Ms. McMurphy talked about with any of them?"

Amity shook her head. "No. They were too far away."

"And were you here yesterday?"

"No. I'm not usually out on a Friday, unless we're going to a show."

"Are you aware of any conflicts Ms. McMurphy might have had with anyone? Or if someone might want to hurt her?"

Besides me? "Not anything specific, no. She wasn't well-liked, seemed kinda shady to me. I have no idea why Jackie hired her. Everybody loved Virginia, but her husband got transferred, so she had to quit. I didn't realize Jackie was *that* desperate to hire a replacement, though."

The detective reached into his breast pocket for a metal business card holder. It had a laser-cut running horse on the front, and Amity couldn't help but smile when he handed her a card.

"That's all I have for now. If you remember anything else, please call me."

Amity walked down the barn aisle with him until she reached Destiny's stall.

"This your horse?"

"Yeah." Amity opened her tack trunk and pulled out a bag of horse cookies.

The mare nickered, her eyes bright and ears pricked forward.

"She's a beauty." Detective Myles ran an appreciative eye over the horse.

"Thanks." Amity doled the treats into the feed bin and the mare began to eat. When Amity put the bag away and turned around, the detective stood on the far side of the aisle with his phone to his ear. She hurried back to sit with Jackie.

The trainer sighed. "I asked Laura to go down the list and call everyone, so they don't come out today. I feel terrible about canceling the Christmas party last minute, but under the circumstances…"

"You sure she can get down the list in time? You know what a gossip she is. I'm sure she'll tell every detail she knows and then speculate about how it happened."

Jackie ran a hand through her dark hair and sighed. "I'm aware. But I just wasn't up to it."

Technicians from the Medical Examiner's Office struggled to roll the stretcher, laden with a black body bag, through the sandy aisleway and toward their van. Amity had wished Diana gone many times during her short employment at the stables, but never like this. Not bludgeoned to death in a horse stall. *When had horse thieves gotten so violent?*

A woman, dressed similarly to Detective Myles, marched over to talk to him. After a brief conversation, she approached Jackie and Amity.

"Forensics is going to be here for some time. If you'd like to go get some lunch or something, you're free to go."

"Thank you." Jackie stood up, her bad knee cracking. "You want to come over to the house with me, Amity?"

"Sure. Can't stay long, though. The dogs are in the car."

The two women left the barn and walked the fifty yards to Jackie's house, past the outdoor dressage area and through the flower-twined arbor gate that separated her yard from the rest of the property.

The wind had picked up, making it uncomfortably chilly to sit on the deck, so they sat in the breakfast nook inside. Jackie poured them each a glass of iced tea.

Amity shook her head. "I can't believe this happened. Just right over there. While you were asleep."

"I know. It's crazy. People steal tack all the time. And sometimes horses. But I've never heard of a barn thief killing anybody."

"Yeah. But I'm wondering why Diana was here so late. Or early." Amity shrugged.

"Faraday was colicky last night. Dr. Lenihan came out and gave him some oil. That got everything moving, and he was fine. She was here until nearly ten. Diana had left to get dinner, but she had saddle pads in the wash, so I assumed she came back to put them in the dryer before she called it a day. That's when she must have... stumbled on the thieves."

"That's another thing." Amity frowned. "Why Flyboy? If they were going to steal a horse, there are a lot more valuable ones than him in the barn."

"Who knows? Could be someone was specifically looking for a big red horse. Or—and I hate to even think about this—they planned on butchering him. It's gotten to be a big problem in Florida. I dread it coming here."

Amity shuddered. That might explain the steel pipe. Quieter than a gunshot. And poor Diana might just have given her life for Flyboy's.

Sunday morning was crisp and cool, without a cloud in the deep blue sky. After a leisurely breakfast, Amity figured that the stables were surely starting to get back to normal. She hadn't had the chance to ride on Saturday, so she was eager to get out and see Destiny.

"Jax! Amber! Come on, pups! Let's go."

The dogs were always happy to go to the barn with her, and they danced around her feet as she grabbed her keys and headed for the door.

When Amity arrived and started down the barn aisle, she noticed Georgia Hamilton standing in front of Flyboy's stall, frowning.

Amity stopped next to her. "Were you close?"

"What?"

"You and Diana. Were you close?"

"No. I barely knew her. I had a strange call from a number I didn't recognize around 5 AM yesterday saying that Flyboy was dead, and they wanted to start an insurance claim."

"What an awful way to get woken up."

"Rolled straight to voice mail—do not disturb was on. When I got up at six, I called Jackie, and she said he'd gotten out, but she was leading him back to the barn even as we spoke. The horse was perfectly fine."

"Huh. Not making any accusations, but have you talked to Kymberleigh? Without her mom around? Perhaps she and some friends were making prank calls."

"Yes. Because calling the insurance agent at 5 in the morning with a bogus claim is hilarious."

Amity shrugged. "Teenagers. Could be they weren't entirely… sober? I don't know. Just an idea. You riding today?"

"Yeah. Gonna take Bailey out for a hack in the cross-country field."

"Want some company?"

"Sure."

"Cool. I'll get Destiny."

Running late for her Tuesday night lesson, Amity hurried down the aisleway. Flyboy wasn't in his stall, but she thought nothing of it, because Kym usually rode him in the group session on Tuesdays.

The lady detective from Saturday suddenly appeared in the stall, giving Amity a start. She must have been leaning over, out of sight.

"Sorry." She crossed her arms and scowled at the bedding.

"Is there something I can help you with?"

"No."

"Okay." Put off by the detective's curt replies, Amity was happy to get ready for her lesson.

Kym had not been there. Jackie said that the girl and Diana had become best buddies, and Kym was still broken up about her death. Flyboy was waiting in the round pen while the detective scoured his stall, but she hadn't been forthcoming about what she was looking for. By the time Amity dismounted after her ride, the detective had left.

Destiny crunched an apple-flavored cookie while her owner brushed away the saddle marks and then some. Amity found that grooming her horse was as soothing to her as it was to the mare.

"You're going to rub all the hair off of her." Jackie leaned against the stall door.

"Soft brush." Amity paused her horse grooming. "What was that detective looking for?"

"Didn't really say, but she was picking through Flyboy's shavings for an hour and sent a couple of co-workers out to sift through the manure pile."

"They find anything?"

"Didn't look like it, but what do I know? I was teaching lessons."

Amity's phone rang, and she slid her hand down her thigh to the snug pocket to retrieve it. "Kathy? What's—"

"Amity! I need your help! I've been arrested for Diana's murder."

Kathy stared out the window of her friend's car. Amity had dragged Martin Kellog, who was both her brother's close friend and a prominent criminal defense lawyer, down to the county jail. He had demanded that the District Attorney charge Kathy or release her, and given the lack of anything but circumstantial evidence, the DA let her go. For now.

Amity stepped on the brakes a little too hard as a yellow light changed to red, jolting both of them against their seatbelts. "I can't get over how Simon just ran off when you confronted him for lying about being at the barn Thursday." She turned to look at her friend. "You don't think he had anything to do with Diana's death, do you? I mean, what if he went to the barn to break up with her and things got out of hand? That could explain his disappearance."

Kathy sniffled. "He wouldn't do something like that."

That's not the same as a no. "I hope you're right. Is there a place he goes when he's upset?"

"I already told the police about our cabin at the lake. There's no landline, and cell reception is spotty at best. They said he wasn't there. Except... they did find his phone in some bushes. I'm worried about him. Sure, I'm angry with him for lying, but... I don't want anything bad to happen to him. He said he was tempted. Diana's half our age and she's been throwing herself at him pretty hard. But he swore up and down that he didn't act on his attraction."

"And you believe him?"

Kathy sighed, and it took her some time to answer. "I honestly don't know." She twisted her wedding band. "I never wished Diana dead. But if I'm totally honest, I'm not shedding any tears over her either. As I told that detective, I seriously doubt she surprised a thief. She'd stomped on a lot of toes and burned a lot of bridges in the short time she's been in town. I'm sure there's no shortage of people who'd be angry enough to do her in."

"Yeah." Amity pressed the accelerator. "That's why I was surprised when Jackie hired her."

"Really? She's all about giving people second chances. She seems to believe that just because her sister was able to get off drugs and get her life back that everybody's problems can be fixed with some friendship fairy dust. Some people are just rotten to the core and there's nothing anybody can do about it, not even with a hundred chances."

The speaker jangled as a call came in. The display read 'Sheriff's Office,' and Amity hesitated to answer, fearing that they were calling to tell her to turn the car around and bring Kathy back.

"Aren't you going to pick up?"

Amity tapped the SUV's touchscreen. "Hello?"

"Ms. Hudson? Detective Myles."

"This is Amity."

"Are you on speaker?"

"Yes."

"I see. Would you please come down to my office this afternoon. I need to ask you a few questions."

"I'm in my car, and I've been out riding, so I'll need a shower. It may be an hour or two."

"That's fine. I'll be here."

Amity ended the call. "What do you suppose he wants?"

"Who knows?"

They pulled into Kathy's driveway. Jax started barking with excitement.

Kathy laughed. "Why don't you stay in the car with the dogs? It won't take long for me to grab an overnight bag."

Amber lay on the couch, her head in Kathy's lap. Jax leaned against the arm of the sofa. Kathy rubbed his ears with one hand and stroked Amber's neck with the other.

Amity pulled her damp hair off her collar. "Looks like you're being well taken care of. Hopefully, this won't take too long, and we can get food delivered when I get back."

"Sounds like a plan."

It took nearly half an hour to get downtown to the sheriff's headquarters, and Amity stewed the whole way. She was angry that they'd arrested Kathy, and wondered if they were as suspicious of Simon as she was. Why else would he be missing? Unless they think Kathy did something to him. But clearly there was no evidence for that, or they wouldn't have let her go. She'd worked herself into a state by the time she pulled into visitor parking.

After she signed in, stepped through the metal detector, and received a visitor badge, Amity had started to cool down. An officer escorted her up to Homicide.

Detective Myles, carrying a manila folder, met her and walked her to an interrogation room.

"Thanks for coming by, Ms. Hudson. I just want to show you a photograph, and I'd like you to tell me if you can identify something."

Amity gritted her teeth and leaned back in the metal chair.

"It's a close-up, just a bruise. It isn't gory."

"Okay."

He retrieved a photo from the folder and placed it on the table in front of her. Amity winced. While she wouldn't describe it as 'gory,' it was still unpleasant to look at. The mark appeared above a flattened eyebrow, and it was an angry red, perhaps an inch wide and only slightly longer. A white, unbruised number three appeared near the end of the injury.

"Is this from the pipe?"

"No."

Amity tilted her head from one side to the other. "You know, it does look like something I've seen before, but I can't place it. Not without context."

He nodded slowly. "I see you got Kathy Edgemont sprung."

"She didn't do anything. You ought to be looking for her missing husband and asking him some questions about what happened to Diana. I'll bet he knows a whole lot more about it than she does."

"Do you think they were lovers, Simon and Diana?"

"Kathy says he swore it wasn't physical."

"But what do *you* think?"

Amity sighed and bit her lip. "I'd like to believe Simon was tempted but faithful, but he couldn't look me in the eye when I saw him on Thursday night. He'd told Kathy he was going out with friends to watch the game, but he was at the barn. With Diana." She glanced at the photo. "It's also true that girl had a lot of enemies. She'd screw people over in a heartbeat. Maybe she just picked the wrong person to victimize."

"Like Jackie Barber?"

"What?"

"Ms. Barber told us that not only did Diana steal $500 in cash from her, but she had started bad-mouthing her to clients. That's what she confronted her about on Thursday evening. Were you aware of this?"

Amity blinked. "No. I didn't hear what was said, and Jackie never mentioned it. But that does explain some things."

"Oh?"

"Yeah. She had been spending a lot of time with Kymberleigh Fields, the owner of the horse in the stall where you found Diana. Kym was still doing Tuesday night group lessons, but she'd started taking private lessons with Diana on Saturdays instead of Jackie. I can totally see Jackie kicking Diana out, but not… not *killing* her. You don't know Jackie. She's the kindest, most soft-hearted person on the planet."

"Were you aware that Jackie Barber served time for aggravated assault when she was 19?"

Amity's mouth gaped open. "I… I had not heard that. She was big into giving people second chances, but we all thought it was because her sister was a junkie who managed to get clean. I had no idea."

"Well, if it makes you feel better, she beat her sister's drug dealer boyfriend with a baseball bat. Put him in the hospital."

Do baseball bats have a number three carved on them? "That just shows how protective she is of the people she loves."

"Yes. Yes, it does." The detective tucked the photo back into its folder. "Thank you for coming by, Ms. Hudson. I'll see you out."

"Ugggh." Amity spat dog hair out of her mouth. "Amber! Get off me."

The big dog's tail flopped in her face again. Amber sat resolutely between Amity and the window. Jack's low growl rumbled in Amity's chest.

A man's silhouette loomed outside behind the sheer curtain. Slowly, the window started sliding open. Amity's heart pounded against her chest and her mouth went dry.

"No!" She jumped out of bed, tripping over Jax and catching herself on the wall before she slammed the window closed and locked it.

Amity grabbed her phone and ran. "Kathy! Kathy, get up!"

She burst into the guest room. Kathy was sitting up in bed, rubbing her eyes. "What—"

"Get in the closet!" Amity grabbed her friend's arm and dragged her out of bed.

"I don't—"

"Shhh! Closet! Now!"

The two women bundled into the mostly empty closet and Amity pulled the folding door shut behind them. She fumbled with her phone and dialed 9-1-1.

"Yes. We need help! Someone's trying to break into the house!"

Kathy gasped.

Amity gave the operator her address and stayed on the line.

In the master bedroom, Jax barked and snarled like a wild thing. "If he hurts my dogs..."

It felt like hours, cowering in the closet, the dog going crazy in the next room. Both women jumped as a loud knock sounded on the front door. "Police!"

Sighing with relief, Amity pushed open the closet and crawled out. Scrambling to her feet, she shut the dogs in her bedroom and hurried to let the officers in. Kathy trailed behind her.

"Just a minute!" Amity peered through the peephole. Red and blue lights strobed outside. She opened the door.

"Miss Hudson?"

Before Amity could answer, Kathy shouted, "Simon!"

"You know this guy?" The officer turned his head toward a man in handcuffs near the patrol car.

"He's her husband."

Kathy adjusted her nightgown and rushed to Simon's side.

"Kathy? I'm sorry! I had to talk to you, but I didn't think Amity would let me in."

"So you tried to break into my house?" Amity shook her head, incredulous. "You couldn't just call your wife?"

"Lost my phone at the cabin."

Kathy began to cry when the police put Simon in the back of the car. The officers took a report and headed downtown. Amity sighed as she got dressed. The last thing she wanted to be doing at three in the morning was bailing Simon Edgemont out of jail.

"I tried calling, but I couldn't get through." Jackie came down the barn aisle to meet Amity.

"Yeah. I thought my phone was on the charger, but it wasn't."

"Destiny threw a shoe. Farrier'll be out in the morning."

Great. "Oh, well. Had to bring your Christmas gift out anyway. Isn't there some weather coming in later?" Amity handed over a sparkly gift bag.

"Thank you so much! Yours is in the office. Weatherman says there's a wintry mix headed our way, so you might want to go hunt up that shoe. Don't want Destiny to step on it. She was fine going out to her paddock, but was off coming back in. Must be in the turn out."

Amity zipped her coat all the way up and headed toward Destiny's paddock. The hasty north wind was pushing a wall of grey-blue clouds toward the barn, and its icy fingers played with her hair.

It didn't take long to find the iron horseshoe in the mud next to the water trough. *Damn gumbo.* It was hard to understand how the black clay could be both extremely slippery and extremely sticky at the same time.

She picked up the shoe, careful to turn it so the loose nails stayed in their grooves and didn't fall to the ground. She took three steps toward the gate and froze.

Yanking her phone out of her pocket, she opened the call log and hit a number.

"Detective Myles."

"Amity Hudson. I know who killed Diana."

Still dressed in her riding gear, Amity again sat in the metal chair in the interrogation room.

Detective Myles eyed the muddy horseshoe suspiciously. "Okay. Whodunnit?"

"You remember that I told you Kymberleigh Fields had started shifting her lessons over from Jackie to Diana? Her horse, Flyboy lives in the stall where Diana was found."

"Okay. Are you saying Kimberleigh did it? Why?"

Amity shook her head rapidly. "No. Not at all. Kim and Flyboy were not a good match, but Kym's mom was in love with that horse. No way she was going to let her daughter sell him. They had plenty of money, so I don't understand why they didn't just buy Kym another horse."

"So, you suspect Kym's mother killed Jackie? Was the trainer pressuring Kym to sell the horse?"

"She might have been. But there was the strange phone call that Georgia Hamilton got at five o'clock on Saturday morning."

"And Georgia Hamilton is…?"

"She's an agent for an equine insurance company, and she just happens to ride at our barn. She told me that someone called her the morning Jackie died and left a voice mail saying that Flyboy was dead, and they needed to file a claim. But he was just fine. In fact, Jackie found him roaming around with a halter and lead on. That's why she thought someone might have been trying to steal him, and Diana walked in on them."

The detective's brow furrowed.

"Flyboy knows how to untie knots, and he can do it pretty quickly. I told you how shady Diana was. I'm one hundred percent certain that she walked into his stall with that steel pipe to break his leg so Kym would have to put him down. She could then buy a new horse with the insurance money. She didn't count on Flyboy untying the lead and defending himself by kicking her in the face. See?"

Amity pushed the horseshoe over to the detective and pointed to the edge. The number three was debossed into the metal near the end.

"Flyboy wears a size three shoe."

Detective Myles picked up the shoe and examined it. "Is this his?"

"No. Destiny's."

"Okay. We'll collect his shoes and see if we have a match. But what does Diana get out of this? Insurance fraud seems like a big risk to take when she doesn't even get the payout."

"If she connects Kym with a seller, she gets a finder's fee. And I'm sure she already had horses lined up for Kym to try. That, and any clients she could steal from Jackie."

The detective looked down at the shoe and sighed. He got to his feet. "Thanks for coming in. Happy holidays, Ms. Hudson."

Amity rose and picked up her horseshoe. "Happy holidays, Detective."

She grinned. Knowing none of her friends was a killer was the best Christmas present ever.

Roast Beast

By A. B. Richards

FATHER had spent the entire day hunting. Animals of any kind are hard to find in the winter, much less those perfect for the feast. But the two he'd managed to harvest were well fed, with meaty, succulent drumsticks. Fat sizzled as it dripped into the open flames and Father's mouth watered, anticipating the savory, juicy meat.

The resinous scent of evergreens hung heavy in the forest. Frigid, crisp air chilled hands and bit noses, but it wasn't cold enough for snow.

This was Father's favorite time of year. When the wheel turned, and the sticky summer gave way to cooler fall, then turned again to silent winter. He was built for the chill. It wouldn't be long now before the relatives began arriving, arms loaded with food and gifts. They always spent these longest of the winter nights together in celebration.

Father moved a backpack out of his way and rotated the spit.

The feast had come and gone. Father stooped at the sign posted near the trailhead. It was not his language, and he could not read the symbols that appeared above the image, but he assumed it was a tribute to the dead. Whatever they meant, the symbols were always the same.

He paused for a moment of silence. Father was deeply grateful to the bounty of the forest, and thanked the animals who gave their lives for the sustenance of his family.

These delicate creatures came often to his woods and in greater numbers lately, and he was thankful. He had to do his part to thin the herd. Picking off the weak kept the rest healthy. Poor things were often not strong enough to survive in nature on their own, after all. Not without protection for their tiny feet, and the shelters and food they carried in with them.

Father set the backpack down underneath the sign and smoothed the thick hair on his chest where the straps had been. He again thanked them for their sacrifice and strode back into his forest.

MISSING

DAN AND JULIE FINCH MISSING
SINCE DECEMBER 21.
CALL THE SHERIFF'S
DEPARTMENT IMMEDIATELY IF
YOU HAVE SEEN THEM.

THE BLUE RHINO
By A.B. Richards

G RANSY, where's the knife?"

"Coffee table. You may have to wipe it off."

Winona found the blade, sticky with red clumps. She cleaned it as best she could with a slightly used paper towel. "Wouldn't it have been easier to put the candy in a plastic bag and hit it with a rolling pin?"

Gransy looked up from the box of Christmas ornaments in her lap. "Not the cinnamon ones. They just squish like tiny little pancakes."

"Ah." Winona cut the kitchen twine and tied it off, popcorn garland complete. A true crime podcast played over a smart speaker, providing background noise for holiday preparations.

Gransy frowned at the baubles, set them aside, and picked up another box.

"What are you looking for?"

"You remember last year I went to my 50th high school reunion? And they gave us those blown glass rhino Christmas ornaments with 'Morgan HS Class of 1968' on them?"

"Oh, yeah. It was kinda blue."

Gransy nodded. "I asked your mother to put it in with the other ornaments, and now I can't find it."

"She'll be back from the store soon."

"Oh, my." Gransy put her hand over her mouth as she stared at the speaker.

Winona tilted her head to listen.

"Today is the twentieth anniversary of the disappearance of Kari Williams, an eighteen-year-old Springfield woman. Was she a runaway or a victim of the Millennium Killer?"

"Didn't she use to babysit me? I was in what, fourth grade? fifth? when it happened? I have vague memories of Mom and GPop getting into a big argument about her disappearance for some reason."

Gransy closed the lid on the second box. "Yes. Kari lived just down the street from you. Bernard, God rest his soul, had his own theories about the disappearances, and Ramona found them... disturbing."

The podcast continued. "... at least six other girls who went missing around the same time. Three were found dead and, due to the similarities of their deaths, the Springfield Picayune dubbed the perpetrator 'The Millennium Killer,' since he apparently started in 2000. Kari's parents hired multiple private investigators and kept her name in the news, but they failed to turn up any leads on her whereabouts. The Millennium Killer was never identified or caught. More after the break."

The music that started the commercial was an icy blast from the past. Kari, who was on the award-winning dance team, had taught Winona a dance to her favorite song. The one she played almost on repeat. Winona mouthed the words to 'It's My Life (Don't You Forget)' that had made her feel like one of the cool kids. She'd been so disappointed when her mother told her the version that Kari liked was a cover of a song that was popular when Ramona was in high school. Instead of a fresh, new thing, it had seemed like a hand-me-down. Oh, well. Reduce. Reuse. Recycle.

Winona got to her feet to drape the garland around the tree. "I guess true crime obsession skips a generation. What did GPop say about it that got Mom so angry?"

"As a truck driver, Bernard knew quite a lot about what goes on at truck stops. He figured the missing girls were either runaways looking for rides out of town or lot lizards."

"I'm sorry, what?"

"Hookers who work truck stop parking lots. Anyway, your mother was close friends with Kari's mother at the time and she got real mad that he would paint the girl with that kind of tar."

"…of the three women were strangled with a ligature of some type. Each had burns, possibly from a cigarette, and their hair had been cut. No identification was found, and…."

The podcast outlined the lives of the three young, dead women and the other three known missing in the same area at the time the supposed serial killer was active. Winona was only half listening, but she caught the names Heather and Renee as she climbed on the stepladder to place the angel on top of the tree. She had two coworkers with those names, a Heather in Accounting and a Renee in R&D, and that's likely why they stuck in her brain. Winona felt a moment of sadness for the lost Heather and Renee, cruelly snatched from their families before they had a chance to blossom into adulthood.

Dinging sounded from the next room, and Gransy hurried to the kitchen to take cookies out of the oven. Oliver, her probably poodle mix, jumped down from the couch and shadowed her, nails clicking on the hardwood floor.

The side door opened. "Can somebody help me bring stuff in?" Ramona called.

"Be there in a minute, Mom."

Winona folded the stepladder and carried it with her to the garage. She leaned it against the wall and returned with bags of groceries. Ramona put the food away while Winona made a second, then a third trip.

"What did you girls get up to this afternoon?"

"Finished decorating the tree." Winona nabbed a cookie, blowing on the molten chocolate before she took a bite. Gransy used Mexican vanilla in her choc chip cookies, the kind with a hint of coconut. Made all the difference.

Gransy turned to her daughter. "I sure am glad Winslow was able to get the tree up and run the lights yesterday. Is he going to make it for dinner tonight?"

Ramona shrugged. "Not sure. He messaged me to say there was a chopper on the way from a major car accident, and he expected to be in surgery for a while. Show me the tree."

Winona popped the last of the cookie into her mouth and led the way to the living room. Gransy flipped the wall switch that turned on the twinkling Christmas lights. It wasn't dark outside, but the corner where the tree stood was shadowy and the colored LEDs sparkled and danced in the dim light.

"Looks great! Ready for presents."

"Honey, do you remember where you put that rhino ornament I got last year from my class reunion? I wanted to hang it on the tree."

Ramona scanned the storage containers on the floor. "There was some space in one of the glass ornament boxes, so I tucked it in there. You can't find it?"

Gransy shook her head. "I've been through all of them at least twice."

"I'll go up in the attic and look around. Maybe Daddy forgot to bring it down when he got the others. I mean, the lights take up an entire box just on their own." Winona started toward the attic, then stopped. "Mom? Do you still keep in touch with Kari Williams' mother?"

Ramona tilted her head. "Not really. She moved to DC to join some crime prevention think-tank. We exchange Christmas cards, but that's about it. Why do you ask?"

"Gransy and I were listening to our show—"

"I don't understand the fascination with true crime. Isn't it just depressing, listening to that stuff?"

Gransy and Winona gave each other a knowing look.

"*You* might think so." Gransy waved the cookie spatula, accenting her words. "But when the killers get caught, it just shows there is justice in this world. Gives you a sense of order, and a reminder that while there are bad guys doing bad stuff, there are a lot of good guys taking them down."

Ramona raised an eyebrow. "If you say so, Mama."

Winona resumed her attic errand while her mother and grandmother headed to the kitchen to fix dinner. She pulled on the cord that hung from the hall ceiling and unfolded the stairs. They creaked and wobbled as she climbed up. She reminded herself that if they would support her father's weight, they would support hers. A dusty light switch protruded from a bare 2 x 4 and she turned on the naked bulb.

She hoped to find a forgotten Christmas storage box, but there was no red plastic in sight. Orange and black. Pink and yellow. No red and green.

Scratching came from the corner farthest from the light. Winona whipped her head in that direction. Her pulse quickened as she caught a glimpse of something darting away out of the corner of her eye. Winona swallowed hard and hastily pulled her phone out of her pocket and turned on the flashlight. Nothing moved, and she told herself that the shadow and the scratching must have been a mouse.

She noticed that the lid on an old wooden steamer trunk was slightly open. Was that where the mouse was hiding? Winona ducked her head and shuffled to the trunk to inspect the damage from the gnawing rodent.

When she opened the top, the yellowed papers and old photos appeared untouched. She smiled at a picture of Gransy and GPop as a young couple. She had always been very close with her grandmother, but GPop was gone a lot with his job, and she hadn't had nearly as strong a connection with him.

It didn't help that he'd died suddenly, the summer between fifth and sixth grade. Her father had said that it was a massive heart attack. Unsurprising, given what a heavy smoker he was.

The blue rhino obviously wasn't going to be in the trunk. But curiosity led her down the primrose path. Humming 'It's my Life'—her new earworm—Winona picked up a bundle of letters, bound together with yarn. She untied the bow knot and opened the first envelope, then quickly replaced the note when she realized that they were racy love letters between Gransy and GPop, from back in the day.

There was a scrapbook with some random newspaper clippings and birthday cards GPop had received from his grandkids over the years. Winona had a fair number of cousins, many of whom would soon be arriving at Gransy's house to celebrate the holidays.

Kerchunk. Kerchunk.

Winona jumped at the sound of a loud rattle from the bottom of the trunk. The corner of a metal box peeked out from the old papers.

She worked the shoebox-sized container out from underneath the stack of mementos.

Holding it at arm's length in case a frightened family of rodents leaped out at her, she carefully undid the clasp.

Inside were perhaps a dozen smaller plastic boxes. They were semi opaque and a blob of blue in one from the top row caught her eye.

She opened the lid and gasped as she dropped the box on the floor.

The blue rhino ornament was inside, nestled against a lock of black hair, the cut edge bound with a rubber band. Beneath that was a driver's license.

Winona stared at Kari Williams' photo, the cookie she'd just eaten threatening to rise.

Rest

By Artemis Greenleaf

ALWAYS liked the night shift. Most of the world is asleep and there's a kind of peace when enveloped in Nyx's bosom that even the crickets can't diminish. I've been at this place ten years now, and everyone here is like family.

Who's that you say? That's Mary Anne. She's a little shy. You have to understand—she was in a bad car accident a few years ago, and her face got kinda messed up. But she's sweet as bees' breath and one of my favorite folks. Her husband's on the other side, you see. I usually visit with Mary Anne a little bit between making my rounds.

Security's not a tough job around here. Once in a while, kids will turn up looking to make mischief, but I've never had trouble runnin' 'em off. Don't think they mean any harm, just kids being kids. But this isn't the place for that.

Not sure when I started whistling as I walked my beat. But that's usually all it takes. Trespassers hear me coming and they beat it out of here like scalded haints, to the front gate, if they're smart. Most of the time.

There's that one guy... He stands in the street in front of the gate, wearing a fedora hat. Don't like him, but he doesn't come on the property. Just stands there in the road, so not much I can do about it.

I'd be more worried if he came from the woods at the back of the place. Lot of wildlife back there, and I'm not sure all of it is something you'd find in a science book. But maybe that's just me. Some hikers found a body in there a few years ago. Never did identify that poor girl, what was left of her, anyways.

Best not to go out into the trees. No real reason to. As long as you stay inside the fence, you'll be fine. And… if you see a deer come out of the forest, a big black one? Don't pay it no mind. Some folks say it talks to them. Just ignore it. Don't look at it or touch it. And obviously, don't speak to it.

Christmas is comin' up. Best time of the year. Lot of folks comin' by, so keep your eyes peeled for thieves.

Coming up on Building D. The art déco one? I will warn you the people there are not too friendly. But they won't bother you if you don't bother them. Usually. If you ever hear a baby crying from there, just keep walking. It isn't a baby.

You getting all this down? My wife's gonna be here before long to pick me up. Don't worry—you'll get the hang of it. I will miss this place, don't get me wrong, but I'm tired. More than ready to retire and take a good long rest.

This is the equipment storage building. Backhoe, mower, lawn tools, that kind of stuff. Normally, it's locked up tight. Looks like that door's ajar, don't you think?

A side door flies open and a wild man with a machete raised over his head stands in the doorway. His clothes are dirty, stained, and ill-fitting. Greasy, unkempt hair brushes his shoulders and a bushy, ungroomed beard hangs to his chest.

"Easy there, Byron. It's just me. Me and my trainee. I'm retiring. Did I tell you?"

No idea what his real name is. I just call him Byron because he's mad, bad, and dangerous to know.

The man lowers the blade and grunts.

"There was an employee potluck Christmas party today. Plenty of food in the office. I unlocked the door for you."

A little girl appears next to him. I haven't asked how old she is, but thinking back to when my own kids were young, I'm guessing she's around seven.

"Hi, Sarita." I smile at her. She's very shy, and nearly as filthy as the man. She ducks behind him.

What's that? You've seen her on TV? Huh. Couldn't tell you the last time I sat down and watched the news.

Yep. That makes sense, seeing he's on the lam. Doesn't want to be arrested for killing her mom. How much is that reward?

Fifty thousand? I whistle. That's a good chunk of change. Byron could get his life back on track with that money. If they don't throw him under the jail.

No, no, no. You got the wrong end of the stick. I didn't say *he* killed her mother. She was definitely murdered, though. He was there, and he ran away with her kid. Look at him—will a jury believe that story? Do you think he can afford a high-priced lawyer to keep him off death row? He's got a record as it is, so why wouldn't they lock him up and throw away the key?

I know because he told me. And look at Sarita—if she'd watched him kill her mother, don't you think she'd be terrified of him?

Yes, I've heard of Stockholm syndrome. They've only been here a few days, though. Trying to lay low, stay outta sight of both John Law and the gang that killed Sarita's mom.

I shrug. Criminal enterprise isn't different from any other kind of capitalism. It's all in the product they sell. Some people want to buy kids. A lot of addict moms will sell theirs for their next fix. Sarita's mom wouldn't. So they killed her, but Byron grabbed Sarita and ran. He'd been friends with her mom, almost since she hit the streets.

Byron and Sarita start toward the office.

You're right. We've got to do something. The streets are no place for a seven-year-old girl. Especially not in winter. Let's go back to the office with them. After they eat, we'll talk about it with Byron.

A baby wails.

Looks like something else is hungry, too.

Yes, Building D. I told you.

Byron pauses and starts toward the door, which should absolutely not be open. I rush over, blocking his way.

"Stay out of there."

Byron scowls and raises his machete. "There's a baby...."

"Look closer, but do not cross the threshold."

He steps almost on top of me and peers into the gloom, then jumps back.

I raise my hands, palms up. "Do babies have glowing red eyes?"

Shaking his head, he grabs Sarita's hand, and they jog toward the office and slip in through the back door.

I scout for silverware while Byron and Sarita wash up. Byron chooses dishes from the refrigerator, then serves up plates to heat in the microwave.

It does my heart good to see them having a good meal. Afterward, Sarita helps him tidy up.

"You know, the tipline is anonymous. And there's a big reward for Sarita's return."

Byron looks down and strokes the girl's tangled hair.

"They threw her mom out. What's to keep them from doing the same to Sarita?"

"She should be in school, not begging on the streets. The reward's $50,000."

Byron laughs bitterly. "Do I look like I have a bank account?"

What's that? Good idea.

"Write a letter explaining what happened. Name names, if you can. Sarita'll corroborate your story, won't she? Cash reward...."

Sarita tugs on Byron's ragged jacket. "Can we stay in here? It's nice and warm."

"Of course, sweetie."

Byron sighs and goes off in search of paper. When he returns, he sits at the breakroom table, the ballpoint pen scratching across the pages for some time. When he's done, he folds them into thirds and stuffs them into an envelope, which he addresses to 'Police.'

He gives Sarita a sad smile. "It's going to be okay, sweetheart. You have to go back to your family. They miss you a lot. The police will ask a lot of questions. Just tell the truth."

She throws her arms around him. "Are you coming with me?"

"Not just yet."

"But you will come?"

"I'll do my best."

Sarita looks sad, but she doesn't cry.

Byron goes to the phone hanging on the wall, picks up the receiver, and punches three digits.

Red and blue flashing lights wash over the brick building and dead grass. Officers carry Sarita, wrapped in a blanket, out to an ambulance.

"Now that she's safe, you'd better scram, Byron. You know they'll search the place. You did the right thing. Sarita'll be home for Christmas. That's the best gift you can give her."

He slips silently into the night.

Two officers with flashlights head toward us. One is shaking his head.

"What kind of weirdo leaves a kid at a cemetery?"

The other shrugs. "At least she's safe."

They pass us by with no notice.

You think you got everything?

I hope so, too. Don't worry. You'll get the hang of it.

It's time.

I drag my hand across my headstone, my name chiseled in bold, black letters.

There she is. She's radiant. It's been ten years since I last held her. I open my arms and she hurries toward me.

"Whoa, there, Carol!" I catch her as she stumbles over a pile of earth in front of me. She'd been in hospice, so they were ready to start digging as soon as they got the word from our daughter.

"You want to stay for the funeral? I came to mine. Very touching. You did a good job."

She beams. "No. I just want to go. I'm *so* tired and I need rest."

"Your wish is my command."

I take her hand. The air in front of us splits open and blinding light pours out. Smiling, we step inside.

Survivor

By A. B. Richards

I FELL in love with Timothy Carter the first day of middle school. I was in a panic because I couldn't find the art room. He had walked me there, even though it made him late for math class.

How could I not be smitten? He was kind, smart, and funny, with large grey eyes and curly blond hair. His eyes held secrets, though, and his smile was never wide, as if it were weighed down by some deep and heavy sadness. It wasn't very surprising, given that he had moved in a few doors down with his aunt and uncle over the summer. I had heard that his parents were dead but didn't know the details. He never talked about it. Another quirk he had was that he wouldn't tell me when his birthday was. Said they didn't celebrate. I thought it might be a religious thing, so I didn't push it.

The summer between eighth and ninth grade, as we were going from being the oldest kids in middle school to the youngest kids in high school, was a summer of changes, physical, educational, and emotional.

Then Timothy told me his secret.

It was the night of his eleventh birthday. His family—mom, dad, and two younger sisters—were planning to meet up with his aunt, uncle, and cousins at a restaurant. When the birthday boy's family didn't show, and no one was answering her phone calls, the worried aunt went to the house.

Timothy said he was putting on his shoes when he heard screaming downstairs, then a couple of popping noises, and everything went quiet. When it sounded like more than one person was running up the stairs, he hid in the closet. His parents never ran up the stairs, so in his eleven-year-old brain, it couldn't be them.

Timothy had hidden behind the hanging clothes and didn't see a thing. But he did hear doors opening and closing. His sisters' terrified shrieks. More popping. Footsteps going down the stairs. A door slamming. Then nothing until his aunt came in.

She probably wishes she had just called the cops. Inside, she found her sister and brother-in-law dead on the floor in the living room, dressed for the party. The two girls had been shot to death in their bedroom. The aunt would never have found Timothy if he hadn't opened the closet door when he heard her calling his name.

My heart broke for him, and it made me feel even more protective. He'd been through so much. Timothy told me that his therapist helped a lot. He missed his parents and sisters, but the psychologist had helped him sort through his grief and survivor's guilt.

He wanted to tell me this because he thought I should know. It might help me understand why he was the way he was. Also, the perpetrators were never caught, and the reason for the massacre was never discovered. Nothing was taken, other than lives. His dad worked as a bank manager and his mother was a florist. There seemed to be no reason for the murders.

The killers hadn't come for him over the last three years. But that didn't mean they wouldn't ever. He thought I should be aware. Just in case.

He told me this, sitting in his room where he had a Lego Razor Crest kit put together and prominently displayed on his shelf. He had begged for it for six months, but his parents always said no, and he was heartbroken each time. A week after the murders, he opened his birthday presents, and there was the kit. The thing he'd wanted so badly. He'd put it together, then never touched it again, leaving it as a kind of shrine. I found it beautiful and heartbreaking.

Even though his parents didn't leave him by choice, he still struggled with abandonment issues. Poor thing. Made him a little clingy and insecure, but I understood where he was coming from.

I did my best to make him feel better, but I drew the line at him critiquing my clothes and suggesting what I should wear. Told him that was not gonna fly, and he mostly dropped it. It did mean, though, that he took up almost all my free time, and my friends were a little upset I didn't get together with them much outside of school. But I knew Timothy was emotionally fragile, and he needed me more than they did. It wasn't like I'd moved to Antarctica or something. I still saw them just about every day.

When Brett Samuels' tires got slashed, I can't believe they went so far as to blame Timothy. The football quarterback, and self-described 'Alpha Male,' Brett had asked me out, right in front of Timothy. I told him no way, I had a boyfriend, and that was the end of it. The tire incident happened during the night, and Timothy was with me. Well, we were texting, not actually together.

Timothy never said a word about Brett, and why would he? Brett shot his shot, I blocked it, and that was that. Besides, I think he only asked me out because I was one of the few girls he hadn't slept with, not because he was interested in me particularly.

Personally, I think Brett slashed his own tires, so he could try to pin it on Timothy and make him look bad as revenge for me turning him down. That rejection was a hit to his massive ego, and he didn't know how to handle it. Some people carry spite way too far.

It was winter break our senior year in high school. Timothy and I had applied—early decision—to all the same colleges. But neither of us got into the same schools. It was a bummer, but there were two that were at least in the same city. We talked about getting an apartment together halfway between the universities. But that wasn't easy. He was eighteen but I wasn't, not for a few more months, anyway. He was still in favor of declining the early acceptances and reapplying elsewhere. I had been accepted to my dream school, so I didn't want to do that.

Timothy and I had been together so long that his family was like my family. I was at his aunt's house for a big Christmas party. There were some woods behind the subdivision, part of a big park where we often went to hang out. We went there after lunch, just to get out for a little while.

I'm not sure which cousin it belonged to, but they had a pistol. Whole family was big into target shooting. It was probably their dad's, and I didn't ask if he knew they had it. We took turns shooting at random stuff. Dirt clods. Trees. A Gatorade bottle left lying beside the trail. Timothy was the best shot of all of us, though, and he showed me how to line up the sight. By the time we ran out of bullets, I wasn't too bad, either. Well, at least I was better than when I started.

When we got back to the house, I went to help out in the kitchen before the guests started arriving. Timothy's uncle took him and the cousins to the store for some last-minute items.

As we chopped vegetables, his aunt asked me about plans after graduation, Bunch of other stuff I don't really remember. Then she said something that hit me in the feels.

"You seem to be such a good influence on Timothy. I'm so happy you're in his life."

"Oh. Thank you. He can be a lot, but he's really worth it."

"Yes. He really seems to have gotten his anger management issues under control."

"He must have, because I have never once seen him get mad about anything."

"Dr. Edwards says he's made substantial progress. I think you have a lot to do with it."

"I would hope he's made progress in eight years."

She thought for a moment. "No. More like ten. He started seeing Dr. Edwards in third grade. He was eight or nine."

She changed the subject. I didn't mind. I'd just assumed that Timothy had started seeing Dr. Edwards *after* the murders. But I had never asked. Anyway, water under the bridge.

The party was mostly adults, so after we ate, us kids went upstairs to play video games. Out of the blue, Serena, who was a year younger than us, asked Timothy if he ever thought about what his sisters would be like now. If he missed his parents.

"No."

A single word that made my blood turn to ice. The terrifying smile on his lips. The flat, dead eyes. Like there was no life behind them.

Like a psychopath.

Timothy got up without a word and stalked out of the room.

Suddenly, all the clues I'd so blithely ignored came crashing down on my head. The controlling behavior. The lack of emotion.

The Lego wasn't a shrine. It was a trophy. I knew why the police hadn't found the killer. They were looking for someone outside the house. They'd never found the gun because Timothy still had it.

Trying to keep panic out of my voice, I said to the cousins, "Hey guys? Let's go downstairs. Now."

"But—"

"Now! Hurry, before Timothy comes back."

We ran through the jack-and-jill bathroom and out through another bedroom. I was at the back of the pack, so as I heard the first bedroom door open, I ducked into a closet and hid behind the clothes, waiting for the sounds of popping.

Red Rider

By A. B. Richards

WHAT's wrong with the horses?" Zebulon McCandless peered out the window of the cookshack.

"Cougar? Bear? Best go check it out." Erasmus Sweeney sprinkled more cumin into the large pot of chili and stirred.

The shotguns were all in the main house, and Zeb didn't have time to limp up there and get one. He pulled his revolver from its tooled leather holster and swore under his breath. If it was a bear, the noise from the pistol might frighten it away, but if push came to shove, he didn't think he could fire the single action Colt Peacemaker fast enough to take down a charging bruin.

The four horses in the corral were on high alert—heads raised, ears pricked forward, and nostrils flaring. One or the other of them would snort and the whole group would bolt to the opposite end of the pen. Again and again.

"Phew!" Zeb's nose wrinkled in disgust. Whatever was spooking the horses smelled like a wet dog strapped to a billy goat, and both of them soaked in piss.

"Hey!" He made his voice as gruff as he could. "Get outta here!" It was all bluff and bluster—his broken leg had healed to the point he could hobble around without crutches, but he was nothing like fit for fight or flight.

Zeb continued his circuit of the corral until he came across some odd tracks in the soft mud. They looked similar to elk but were twice the size. He'd seen a taxidermied moose at a museum in Phoenix once, but those giants lived hundreds of miles to the north. Unless one hopped a steam train, he didn't see any way a moose would be wandering around the Dunn Ranch in Arizona.

His gaze followed that of the horses. Twilight hung thick over the bleak Superstition Mountains to the north. It was already night in the canyons, while the dying sun painted the jagged bones of the mountains red.

Something large moved in the half-light, but he couldn't tell what it was. The important thing was that it was moving away from the ranch, and quickly, to boot. He considered shooting at it, but it was already out of range. No need to waste a precious bullet.

Still watchful, the horses had begun to settle. Zeb cast a longing look toward the main house. He had eyes for Adalynn Dunn, but Teddy Dunn would never let a common ranch hand court his daughter. Zeb would probably be horsewhipped if Teddy had the faintest inkling the cowboy entertained such carnal thoughts about her. The red velvet Christmas bow on the front door was a cheery invitation. But not for Zeb.

He continued his trek around the corral but found nothing noteworthy. The horses were back at their hay, chewing as if nothing had happened. He strapped the revolver back in its holster and hurried back to the cookshack.

"Well?" Razzy asked, pulling a pan from the oven of a wood-fired cookstove.

"If I didn't know better, I'd say it was a moose."

Razzy chuckled. "Well, ya took a hard knock to yer noggin the other day."

Zeb shrugged. "It was bigger'n an elk and stank like the Devil, whatever it was." The toasty aroma of warm biscuits hit his nose, and he wanted to stop talking and eat.

Razzy stepped to the doorway to clang the dinner bell.

A posse of a dozen men thundered up the ranch road around midday. Zeb and Razzy left their dinner on the table and came from the cookshack to meet them.

Morris Bennett, tin star pinned to his chest, waved toward the house. "Get Mr. Dunn."

"He ain't here." Razzy shook his head. "He and Miss Adalynn went into town. What's the trouble?"

"Can we water the horses?" A man Zeb didn't recognize at the tail end of the group asked.

"Shore." Razzy waved toward the corral and most of the riders urged their horses in that direction.

Morris looked down at Zeb and Razzy. "Florence Marcus got kilt this morning puttin' out her laundry. We're lookin' for the sombitch who dunnit. Gotta be Irish McGilicuddy—there was some red hair snagged on a sage bush near the house."

"Cain't be him." Zeb frowned. "His wife took sick and he carried her to the doctor's in Pheonix. Barely had time to get there, much less come back. Besides, why do you think he'd go and do a thing like that?"

The deputy twisted in his saddle to look at his men. "It was done outta sheer meanness. Somebody beat that poor widda woman to death, all while her daughter was tendin' the chickens."

Razzy scoffed. "Ya know ole Crawford Brooks runs Hereford cattle, and he's the next spread over. You sure that red hair ain't from one of them?"

"I never seen no hair like that on a steer. You keep a lookout now, be on your guard. Who knows where this lunatic'll hit next?"

Morris trotted his horse over to the trough, where the grey gelding sniffed at the water but refused a drink. The posse wheeled around and charged back down the road.

"I guess when the rest of 'em get back from ridin' the fence line, we'll give 'em the news. Isn't Tiny sweet on Miz Florence's daughter?" Razzy stared after the dusty cloud that drifted in their wake.

"That he is. Maybe Miss Adalynn will see fit to invite her to stay until they track down this fella. Far as I know, the Marcus women only had kin back east somewhere."

"Hell of a thing to have to bury your mama the day before Christmas Eve." Zeb leaned against the corral fence as he and a lovestruck Tiny watched the Dunns and a black-clad Lizzie Marcus disembark from the carriage that had pulled up at the main house late in the afternoon.

Tiny lowered his gaze, lest Mr. Dunn catch him staring. "True enough. But after Miss Adalynn lost her mama to the cholera summer before last, she's the best one to help Lizzie. Knows just how that river runs."

The two men had drawn the first watch of the night, starting right after their supper. As soon as the door closed behind Mr. Dunn, Tiny hustled after the carriage. Luke—he always drove for Mr. Dunn—would put the carriage away and Tiny would take care of the horses. Zeb's leg ached, so he limped to the bunkhouse to rest it and, if he was lucky, grab forty winks before Razzy rang the dinner bell.

Tiny paused to stare through the plate-glass window to where Adalynn and Lizzie sat together on the loveseat in the parlor, Adalynn rubbing Lizzie's back. Kerosene lamps lit the room with a cozy glow.

Zeb opened his mouth to crack wise, but a snort came from the corral, snatching both their attention.

There it was again. The putrid reek of wet dog-musk-ammonia.

Tiny gagged. "Ugggh. What the—"

A wet, shuddering growl pierced the darkness, freezing the men where they stood.

The waxing moon had slid part way over the rugged shoulders of the mountain, bleeding silver light on the plain below. The shadowed form of a huge animal, a man on its back, approached the corral. The beast let out a long, croaking groan.

The horses raced back and forth in terror. Tiny ran toward the thing, his lantern bobbing with each stride. Zeb followed as best he could but was much slower. By the time he caught up, Tiny's lantern cast a dull circle on a shaggy red animal.

Zeb raised his lantern to see what kind of man would sit astride this fetid beast. The air left his lungs as if someone had punched him in the gut.

The rider was dead. Had been so for a long time. His blackened skin was stretched over his dry bones, although the white showed through in a lot of places. A shirt had mostly rotted off of him and his dungarees were in tatters.

Tiny broke the silence. "What the hell is a camel doing in Arizona?"

"US Army tried usin' 'em in the desert. My uncle told me about it—he was in the Camel Corps. They were doin' good, until the war came along and messed everything up. After a while, the army sold off the animals, but a lot of the new owners figgered out camels were not like horses, so they just turned 'em loose to fend for themselves."

"How you reckon that fella got up there?"

Zeb shrugged. "He knows, but he ain't tellin'. We should probably try to catch that camel so we can give that poor soul a proper burial."

The scent of fresh hay must have attracted the animal—it was easily lured into the barn with the promise of food. It took some time for Tiny and Zeb to get close to it, but after it ate, it laid down and they were able to free the skeleton, which had been tied to the saddle with leather thongs.

Zeb felt bad for the camel. The saddle had been on it so long that its skin had started to grow around the cinch. He was able to cut it, but the beast bellowed in pain and spat a foul and slimy wad of hay at him when he tried to remove the embedded cotton strands.

He shouted in surprise and dodged the putrid projectile. "Let's just leave him 'til morning and see what Mr. Dunn wants to do about him. Reckon we—"

"Ze—" An odd popping noise came from Tiny.

Zeb turned to see the skeleton had gotten to its feet. Terror rooted his feet to the ground. It had broken Tiny's neck and started to eat his flesh. It turned its empty eye sockets to Zeb.

What have we done?

With each bite he ripped off Tiny's frame, a fresh patch of skin covered its bones. Zeb finally wrenched his eyes free of the grisly tableau and fled.

He pounded on the door of the main house until a grumpy Teddy Dunn let him in. Several of the ranch hands were on guard duty inside the house, and they held their guns at the ready.

Zeb's frantic story about a wild camel and a skeleton was nearly incomprehensible, as he was so terrified that it came out mostly as gibberish. He finally pulled himself together enough to tell them Tiny was being murdered, probably by the same thing that killed Mrs. Marcus.

Dunn and the armed cowboys marched out the door to put down the evil. The barn door opened and a man stepped out but said nothing.

The rancher turned to Zeb and growled, "I thought you said Tiny was being murdered."

"That's not Tiny!"

"Of course it is. You're drunk, McCandless. Go to bed and sleep it off." He looked at the thing wearing Tiny's skin. "Get him to the bunkhouse so he can sober up."

The thing that wasn't Tiny grinned.

Blood Kin

By A. B. Richards

ICOUGHED and red-hot pain seared through my body. Must have broken a rib. Black smoke boiled up from the sheer drop where my cousin Julie's car had left the road. I hoped I was high enough on the mountain to get a cell signal.

Poor Julie. What an awful way to go.

"9-1-1, what's your emergency?"

"Accident. Cousin's car went off the road."

"Is anyone hurt?"

Slow, shallow breaths moved my ribcage the least. "Yeah. Car's... on fire. Don't think she made it out. My ribs..."

"Stay calm, ma'am. Where are you?"

"Not sure. Not from here. Just drove over a creek. Think it's Route 17. Somewhere between Redfield and Jerusalem." My head started to pound.

"Stay on the line. Help is on the way. What's your name, please?"

"Emily Hanson. My cousin is Julie Stowe. From Redfield." I paused to breathe. "I'm from Houston."

"Okay, Emily from Houston. Tell me what happened."

I yawned, then my breath caught as my ribs expanded. "Sorry. So sleepy."

I could hear her talking to me, her calm voice easing me down the river into the cave of Hypnos, and I just didn't seem to have the will to answer. I lay there on the shoulder of the road, wondering if this was how it would end.

My Aunt Evie was buried yesterday. I'd last seen her a little over three months ago, at our family Christmas get-together. Over the holidays, everybody had said how robust she looked, for a woman of eighty-two, a small bruise here and there notwithstanding. Even so, she had people to run the farm—Silas managed the apple orchards and cider mill, Miranda dealt with the bed-and-breakfast clients, and Lenny took care of the syrup operation. No, not Lenny. He retired right after Christmas. There was a new guy called Blaise, and he was blazin' hot.

A shame, really. He's an employee. Was an employee. He'd had a terrible accident in the sugar shack two days ago and been horribly burned. They'd helicoptered him all the way to Boston, but his chances weren't good. Miranda, who pined after him like a lovesick puppy, said he must have been distracted by Aunt Evie's unexpected demise and made a terrible mistake.

Distracted. Yes, I would agree with that.

I had the sensation of floating. Could I fly? Perhaps I'd soar over to my special spot. I laughed, then groaned. Would the 9-1-1 operator think I was crazy? Could she even hear me as I drifted away? I could tell her about the legend. I'm sure she knew, though. Back in the 1700s French soldiers buried four chests of gold near Bristol. Redfield is close to Bristol, so I guess it counted.

Growing up, I had escaped most of the brutal Houston summers to the cool of Vermont. Nestled in the foothills between Lake Champlain and the Green Mountains, this farm had been in the family for generations. Additions had been kludged onto the original structure over the years, making it a hodge-podge of architectural styles, and I loved this eclectic farmhouse.

I'd found a place as a child—a rocky outcropping that seemed to have wide steps carved into it. I always played there, and even as an adult, it was my special retreat on the farm. This past Christmas, I snowshoed out to my favorite spot. One of the flat rocks gave way as my weight hit it, and I sank into the hole. While digging myself out, I found the first chest. There was far too much snow to conduct a proper exploration. I'd have to wait until spring.

I kept my mouth shut. If word got out... poor Aunt Evie'd be overrun with treasure hunters. Who knew what havoc they'd wreak? I covered the hole with some smaller rocks, then pushed snow over them in the off chance someone wandered by. Best to keep it a secret for now.

Gravel jabbed into my cheekbone, but I let my eyes stay closed. Felt like I was drifting in a field of stars, far, far above this blue marble. Couldn't tell how long. It seemed like both forever and an instant.

The wailing of sirens in the distance caught my attention. I could open my eyes if I wanted to. I just didn't want to. The sirens got louder. So loud! Hurried footsteps on the pavement, on the gravel. Warm hands on my shoulders.

"Hello? Ma'am?"

"1... 2... 3."

The searing pain in my side as the two men rolled me onto my back brought me crashing back to Earth. My eyes fluttered open. Other men stood talking out of my line of sight.

"Ma'am?" The older of the two EMTs asked as they strapped me onto a backboard. "Are you Emily?"

I opened my jaw, but I couldn't seem to remember how to shape my mouth around the words that flowed easily from my brain and pooled behind my tongue. I nodded. Sleepy now. They kept asking me questions. Couldn't they see how tired I was? I wasn't able to answer, even if I wanted to, so I pretended not to hear them. After a lot of poking and prodding, they loaded me into the ambulance. I don't remember much about the trip.

"Emily?"

I peeled my lids off my sticky eyeballs and squinted in the bright light.

A man with slicked-back dark hair stood next to me. "I'm Dr. Popa. How do you feel?"

"Ow."

"I can believe that." He had traces of an eastern European accent. "You've got a grade 3 concussion and two broken ribs. You're going to be just fine, but it will take some time to heal. We'll keep you overnight for observation, but you should be released in the morning. Paperwork says you're from Houston. Is that right?"

I nodded.

"No air travel until you're completely healed. Could be a month, maybe more."

My lips felt like the Mojave Desert. "Julie…?"

"I'm sorry."

Not a surprise, but I needed confirmation.

As soon as Julie had called me to say Aunt Evie was dying, I hopped on a plane to Burlington, then drove down to the hospital in Bristol. I got there too late. Wished I'd been able to say goodbye.

Someone knocked on the door as they opened it. A man in khaki and army green stepped in. As he got close to the bed, the yellow patch on his arm came into focus and identified him as Vermont State Police. He carried a pad of forms attached to a clipboard, and he smelled like fir needles and snow.

"I'm Sergeant Daniel. I'd like to talk to you about the accident."

"I'll send the nurse in with some water." Dr. Popa patted the hand that didn't have an IV in it and left the room.

The trooper ran his eye over the medical equipment. "I'm sorry I have to interview you in the hospital. This should only take a few minutes."

A nurse came in with a big plastic lidded tumbler full of ice water. She set it on the table and left. I grabbed it and greedily sucked almost half of the liquid through the accordion straw. Had to stop when my ribs expanded. It was only water, but it tasted like the nectar of the gods in my parched mouth.

Sergeant Daniel waited until I set the cup down. He pulled a small device from a pocket and clicked a button. "Do I have your permission to record this conversation?"

"Yeah."

"Tell me about the accident, please. Start by stating your name."

I was still having a little trouble with words, but they were coming easier. And the ribs only hurt when I breathed. "Emily. Hanson. 'Vited me to get cheese in J'rslem. Something in road. Jul asked me to move it. Tried to run me down. Jumped out of the way. She sideswiped me. Ran off the road. Over the side."

"Why do you think Mrs. Stowe would try to kill you?"

"Mad. Aunt left me the farm. Not her." Mad enough she and her smarmy husband were going to challenge the will.

He flipped through some pages on his clipboard. "Your Aunt Genevieve Chester? Isn't she Mrs. Stowe's mother?"

"Step." I took another pull on the straw.

"Stepmother?"

"Yes." Aunt Evie had warned me some time ago that the farm that had been in our family since the 1790s would only go to blood kin. Julie might be upset. Be prepared.

"Did it seem unusual that she would be angry with you but still invite you to go shopping?"

"Said she was sorry. Aunt Evie left her… a letter. Jul said she understood." I took a few shallow breaths. Talking hurt. "Olive. Branch."

"That crash was a terrible thing." He unclipped an envelope from underneath the pad and laid it on the table. "Some resources for you."

"Thanks."

The sergeant started to switch off his recorder, then stopped. "There was one thing in the car that was a little strange. When you were riding with your cousin, did you notice a chunk of granite about so big in the car?" He spread his hands to indicate something the size of a large potato.

You couldn't sling a cat without hitting granite in Vermont. I shook my head. "From wreck?"

His turn to shrug. "I hope you feel better soon. We'll talk again before you head back to Houston." Sergeant Daniel gave me a friendly smile before he walked out the door.

Miranda set the bag of paperwork and pamphlets from the hospital on the coffee table. Her eyes were puffy from crying. Told me in the car that Blaise had passed. He'd been cooking maple syrup for most of his life. Couldn't understand how he'd managed to tip the 40-gallon pot of it off the fire and onto himself. Police think he must have tripped over some firewood that had fallen onto the floor. What an awful way to go. Poor Blaise.

"You going to rest in here or go to your room, Em?"

"Don't think… I can make it… upstairs."

Miranda nodded. "The Willow Room's available. Unless... you want to stay in Evie's room."

"No. Couldn't bear... bed she died in."

"It's terrible about Julie. I'm so sorry."

"Thank you." Aunt Evie treated her employees like family, while Julie made it clear that she considered Miranda the hired help. I knew not a single one of that waterfall of tears was for my cousin's untimely demise.

I felt light-headed and lay down on the couch. I had to close my eyes against the harsh light that glared in through the picture window. I imagined Blaise as I'd last seen him, his chiseled jaw... and abs. Sweat glistening on his skin like summer dew drops.

It was late morning, and Julie had gone to make Aunt Evie's funeral arrangements, and I'd slipped out to check on my treasure. I had only started to clear away the debris I'd piled there at Christmas when the growl of an engine stopped me. Getting louder, getting closer. Who was invading my hallowed ground?

A four-wheeler pulled up and a delicious man got out. "May I help you, ma'am?"

"I needed some air. My Aunt Evie just... just died."

His eyes softened. "Oh. You must be Emily. Your aunt was a great lady. I'm Blaise, the new sugarmaker."

Had to distract him away from the rocks before he noticed anything. I took a few steps toward him and started to cry.

He hugged me and stroked my hair. "I'm so sorry."

I felt him craning his head over my shoulder. What had caught his eye? I sniffled. "I feel so alone. She was my only blood relative. Is there someplace we can go to... talk? I just really don't want to be by myself right now."

He let me go. "Course. I'm on my way to the sugar shack with the sap. We can talk there."

Poor Miranda. You really missed out.

The blaring of my phone jangled me out of my nap. What did the Vermont State Police want? Hopefully, it was Sergeant Daniel calling to say they're done investigating. "Hello?"

"Miss Hanson?"

"Yes. This Sergeant Daniel?"

"It is. How're you feeling, ma'am?"

I winced as I shifted on the couch. "Been better."

"I'm sure you have. Ma'am, I have a few follow-up questions so I can close out my report. Need to ask you about the skidmarks."

"What skidmarks?"

"That's just it. There weren't any. I can be there in an hour."

"Of course."

I hurried to the kitchen and pulled down Aunt Evie's recipe book from the top shelf, gasping as my broken ribs shifted. Her blueberry megamuffins were locally famous, one of the most popular items on the bed-and-breakfast buffet. It wouldn't seem at all unusual to have a fresh batch around. I got the pans ready.

I poured eleven of the twelve muffins into their over-sized cavities. Was a tablespoon enough? I used half that for Aunt Evie. But she was elderly, and I wanted to make sure I was far away when she started getting sick. If they'd only known to start IV Vitamin K right away, the internal bleeding might have been stopped, but the treatment takes months, if it works at all. The sergeant probably outweighed her by fifty pounds at least, and he needed to go sooner rather than later. I shook my head. Anything more, and even the extra cup of sugar wouldn't cover up the bitterness.

I ground the blue pellets of the long-acting rodenticide into powder and mixed it into the last muffin. I put the biggest, fattest blueberry in the bunch right in the center, so I knew which one had been doctored. The sergeant probably wouldn't eat a muffin if I just handed it to him. But if I ate one too? I'd even offer one to Miranda for good measure.

Had I messed up? I hadn't thought there would be skidmarks if Julie tried to run me down. Maybe if she'd tried to slam on the brakes before going over the edge? And I had worn gloves when I hit her in the head with that lump of granite. They couldn't get fingerprints off that rock anyway, could they? I'd seriously underestimated the impact of the car. Barely grazed me, but still knocked me over onto the guard rail, where I hit my head on a post. Maybe I should have used a smaller rock on the accelerator.

I was pulling the muffins out of the oven when Sergeant Daniel arrived. Miranda answered the door as I turned the treats out onto the cooling rack. I placed a muffin on each of three small plates, making sure I carried the one with the center blueberry in my right hand and the other two in my left. I grabbed three forks and stepped into the dining room, placing the plates on the sideboard.

"Sergeant Daniel? Miranda? I've just taken some blueberry muffins out of the oven. Aunt Evie's recipe. Come on in here, and we'll have a snack while we talk."

I smiled as I handed him his plate, the shriveled and half-sunken blueberry in the center looking back at me like the eye of Horus. I handed him a fork, then served Miranda. We all sat at the table.

"What was it you wanted to know about the skidmarks, Sergeant?" I broke off a slab of the muffin and put it in my mouth.

He was still chewing.

I clenched my jaw to keep from frowning. Had the milk I'd used in the batter gone off? Would he eat the whole thing if it wasn't up to par? I pretended I didn't notice and stuck my fork into the center of the muffin.

And pulled out the biggest, fattest blueberry in the bunch.

If you enjoyed this book, please consider leaving a review at your favorite book site. Reviews help other readers find and enjoy new books!

To explore more content from Artemis Greenleaf, A.B. Richards, and Holly Dey, please visit BlackMareBooks.com